Praise for Norah McClintock

"John Grisham for teens."
— *Vancouver Sun*

WITHDRAWN

Truth and Lies
" . . . the second book in what one can only hope
will be a multibook series."
— *The Globe and Mail*

Scared to Death
"Buckle up — it's going to be a scary ride."
— *St. Catharines Standard*

"McClintock delivers the goods."
— *Quill & Quire*

Over the Edge
"McClintock . . . delivers a solid mystery. . . . True
McClintock fans will grab a can of pop and gulp
down both story and soda in one nervous sitting."
— *Quill & Quire*

Double Cross
"The climax is fraught with danger and emotion,
and the conclusion is a satisfying end
to a good read."
— *Canadian Materials*

"Lots of suspicious behaviour . . . with a smart,
likeable heroine."
— *Canadian Materials*

The THIRD DEGREE

The THIRD DEGREE

Norah McClintock

Revised edition. Originally published as
The Stepfather Game.

Scholastic Canada Ltd.
Toronto New York London Auckland Sydney
Mexico City New Delhi Hong Kong Buenos Aires

Scholastic Canada Ltd.
175 Hillmount Road, Markham, Ontario L6C 1Z7, Canada

Scholastic Inc.
555 Broadway, New York, NY 10012, USA

Scholastic Australia Pty Limited
PO Box 579, Gosford, NSW 2250, Australia

Scholastic New Zealand Limited
Private Bag 94407, Greenmount, Auckland, New Zealand

Scholastic Ltd.
Villiers House, Clarendon Avenue, Leamington Spa,
Warwickshire CV32 5PR, UK

Cover photo credits page 199

Library and Archives Canada Cataloguing in Publication

McClintock, Norah
[Stepfather game]
The third degree / Norah McClintock.

Previously published under title: The stepfather game.
ISBN 0-439-95761-3

I. Title.

PS8575.C62S84 2005   jC813'.54   C2004-904948-8

6 5 4 3 2 1   Printed in Canada   05 06 07 08 09

To my patient family — Mom, Dad,
Herman, Brooke and Quinn

chapter 1

Brynn threw her whole weight against the heavy metal door. It swung open and clanged against the outer brick wall. Six more weeks. That was all she had to endure. In six more weeks, she'd be sprung from the tyranny of books. She'd be able to spend the summer doing what she wanted instead of always buckling down, always applying herself, waging a constant war for first place — a war that at Earl Barron High involved endless battles against tedium.

Earl Barron wasn't exactly in one of Montreal's best neighbourhoods. Brynn thought most of the teachers it attracted were dinosaurs who didn't realize that the world had changed in the four or five decades since they'd been kids. And if they did know, they didn't care. Or they didn't like kids. Or they were burnt out cases who were teaching there because it was the only job they could get. Like The Weasel.

The Weasel taught history, mostly by standing with his back to the class and copying out entire pages from the history text onto the blackboard, which everyone was supposed to copy into their notebooks, memorize and spit back at him at exam time. He never strayed from the text, and if anyone asked questions, The Weasel accused them of not having read the book and made them copy another chapter into their notebooks.

As Brynn scanned the schoolyard, a boy appeared in front of her like an ambusher from behind a door. One minute, she was looking out over the asphalt, clear across to the chain link fence, scanning the yard, looking for the hank of raven hair that was Chloe's — the next minute, two sky-blue eyes were peering down at her.

"Hi, Brynn," he said.

His voice startled her. It always did. It was deep, as if it belonged to a full-grown man. But he wasn't full-grown, even if he was taller than a lot of adults. He was sixteen years old. Although Brynn was tall herself, she had to tip her head back to stare up at him. She kept her eyes expressionless, as if she were looking at mud. But he wasn't mud, and that made it hard. He was Evan O'Neill.

"So," he said, "what'd Rusnek want?"

Rusnek, the vice-principal. An equal opportunity pain in the butt. Rusnek didn't care what colour you were or what church you went to, or even if you went to one. If you were a kid, he didn't like you. Kids didn't like him, either. The talk was that he'd been a corrections officer before he'd gone into teaching and then into school administration. He reminded Brynn of those big German shepherds the cops used to sniff out shipments of heroin down at the docks. He kept his nose to the ground, sniffing for trouble and the kids who made it.

Brynn stared blankly at Evan. It was none of his business what Rusnek wanted, nor was it likely ever to become his business. Besides, she wasn't the one Rusnek had called down to the office. It was Chloe.

"I'm in a hurry," she said. "I have to get home."

"I'll walk you."

"No, thanks." She was more brusque than she had intended, and suddenly she regretted it. His face had a bruised look. She would never have guessed him capable of such hurt astonishment. But an apology now would just encourage him, and she wasn't about to do that.

She brushed past him. As she took the next few steps, she had the same prickly feeling on the back of her neck that she had whenever she was walking home alone late at night. Is he following me, or isn't he? For a moment her elongated shadow skittered alone ahead of her. Then his fell into place beside it. Some people just don't take a hint, Brynn thought.

She tightened her grip on her school books and quickened her pace. But his legs were so long that he kept up effortlessly. "Look, Brynn, I was wondering . . . " What was it with this guy? A well-placed kick probably wouldn't deter him. "The spring dance is coming up, you know."

No kidding. You'd practically have to live on another planet not to know. There were enormous signs in every stairwell. Judy Winter and Marsha Lincoln had planted themselves behind a table at the entrance to the cafeteria every lunch hour for the past week, selling tickets. Even good old

Rusnek was suffering from dance fever. He made an announcement about the dance every morning over the P.A. system.

"You going?" Evan asked.

"No."

"I mean, because if you don't have a date, well, I wouldn't mind if you'd like to maybe go with me."

Brynn stopped walking and turned and fixed him with a stare. The Medusa stare, Chloe called it. It looked like it could turn you to stone. "That's real big of you, Evan," she said.

Like liquid rising in a thermometer, the blood rose in his face. "Hey, all I meant was — "

"I don't care, Evan," she said curtly. "And I really am in a hurry . . . " She saw Edie Hill standing by the gate leading onto St. Urbain, a bleak expression on her thin, pale face. Brynn raised a hand high up above her head and waved with what she hoped looked like enthusiasm.

"Look, Evan, I gotta run," she said. "I promised Phoebe I'd help her with her homework. Talk to you another time, okay?" She sprinted across the asphalt to where Edie was standing.

* * *

Phoebe slipped a hand into her jacket pocket and ran her fingers over the small, hard candies inside. There were maybe three dozen jellybeans in there, all red. She always saved the red for last. She ached to catch one between her fingers, slip it into her mouth, suck off the hard outer coating, and then chew the soft clear gelatinous lump inside.

But if she took one now, Cindy would want one. And nobody, but nobody, got any of Phoebe Torrence's red jellybeans.

"Shirley Marsh says that Frankie Indelli is going to take her to the prom," Cindy was saying. "She says her mother's going to buy her a dress. A black dress. And her mother's going to take her to the hairdresser and get her hair done specially." Cindy sighed. "Some people have all the luck. Frankie is so hot."

The cutest guy in the eighth grade, that's what he was. Phoebe fingered her jellybeans again. "Hey, you want to do something prom night?" she said. "You and me together, I mean. Maybe we could go to a movie, then you could sleep over at my house. I bet my mom would let us order a pizza." Or, more likely, her mother wouldn't even be home, in which case they could definitely order a pizza. It was pretty hard for her mother to tell her what she could and couldn't eat when she was hardly ever home.

"If I were you," Cindy said, "I'd stay away from pizza." She nodded pointedly at Phoebe's stomach.

"That's baby fat," Phoebe said defensively.

"It's fat," Cindy said. "And fat is fat. I bet if you lost a bit of weight, someone would ask you to the prom."

Phoebe's cheeks burned. "Who said I wanted to go?"

"Well, don't you?" Cindy said.

Phoebe narrowed her eyes. "Why?" she asked. "Are you going?"

"Maybe." Cindy said it like it was some big mystery, like for sure she was going but she didn't want to tell.

Phoebe stared at her. "Who are you going with?"

"I didn't say I was going."

"So you aren't going?"

"I didn't say that, either." Cindy grinned.

Phoebe thought she looked stupid in that bright pink lipstick the colour of bubble gum. No one could wear that colour and not look like a clown. "I bet you're not going," she said.

"You can think whatever you want to think. You'll just have to wait and see."

Cindy was acting like she was in second grade, not eighth.

"You can't possibly be going," Phoebe said. "No one in school is that desperate."

"Is that so?"

"Yeah, that's so."

"In that case," Cindy said, "you can walk home by yourself. I don't want to go to your place. And I certainly don't want to help you with your homework."

"So what?" said Phoebe. "I don't need your help." She stuck out her tongue as Cindy spun around and strode away. Phoebe watched her disappear around the corner, her skirt flying. Then, glad that Brynn and especially Chloe were nowhere in sight, she dug her hand into her pocket, pulled out half a dozen jellybeans, crammed them into her mouth all at once and swallowed them, hardly chewing. They tumbled in so many small lumps into the pit of her stomach.

* * *

Chloe groaned. "Are you sure?" she said.

"Yup. There's no doubt about it," Rita said. "You're being followed."

"Don't tell me. Not him again."

Rita grinned. "Uh-huh. Him again. Your not-so-secret admirer."

"What is wrong with that guy?" moaned Chloe. "He follows me everywhere. He came up to me in the cafeteria today, you know, when I was holding a seat for you. He said he'd be honoured if he could take lunch with me. Honoured! To *take* lunch, not eat it. I told him to take a short walk off a long pier. He's so out of it, he didn't have a clue what I was talking about." It was so annoying. She didn't like the guy. She had never offered him the slightest encouragement. In fact, she had gone out of her way to avoid talking to him. "Is he still there?"

Rita glanced around. "Yup."

"Why me? Why doesn't he pick on someone else?"

"Stick with his own kind, you mean?" Rita grinned. "Maybe he figures you are his kind. I mean, it would be an honest mistake."

Chloe's fists began to clench at her sides. She hated it when Rita said things like that. *An honest mistake.* What was that supposed to mean? Just because she had long straight black hair and almond-shaped Asian eyes, and just because her last name was Yan, was that supposed to make it okay for some stupid Chinese guy right off the plane to follow her around everywhere like a puppy dog? He was always smiling — which was even more annoying — and half the time no one could figure out what he was saying, his accent was so thick.

Rita was looking at her with her head tilted a little to one side, big grassy-green eyes soaking Chloe up like a sponge. It didn't take much to imagine her saying to Den, "Hey, you should have seen the look on Chloe's face when I told her the guy has the hots for her." And Den just killing himself laughing. And Shadd smiling in that way of his, so you didn't really know what he was thinking. That was the part that was really killing Chloe. What Shadd would think.

"I ought to just tell him to go blow it out his ear," said Chloe.

"Yeah," said Rita, like it was the best idea she had ever heard. "Yeah, why don't you?" She giggled. "He probably wouldn't have a clue what you were talking about, though. How do you say that in Chinese?"

Chloe hated it when Rita said stuff like that too. At school, the teachers were always saying don't judge a book by its cover. But it seemed to Chloe that's exactly what everyone she knew did. Just because of the way she looked, people were always asking her stupid questions like, "How long has your family been in Canada?" or, "Did you leave because of the Communists?" The one she hated most was, "Say something in Chinese." One of these days she was going to ask one of the Hong Kong kids to teach her a choice phrase, something really crude. Then the next time someone asked her to say something, she would repeat it sweetly, and just as sweetly offer the translation.

She wasn't Chinese, and she hated having to explain it all the time. She was just a person who happened to look Chinese. It was all her father's fault, and she'd never even met him. He had been a student, working his way through university waiting tables at a Chinese restaurant, when he met Chloe's mother, Sheila. Sheila had become pregnant. Six months later, before Chloe was even born, her father went back to China to visit his family. He never returned. A year later Chloe's mother married Philip Torrence, who would become Phoebe's father. Soon after Phoebe was born, he left too. Ever since Chloe could talk, it seemed, people had been coming up to her and saying, "Say something in Chinese." How many times did she have to say it — I have never been to China, I have never even wanted to go to China, I don't know anything about China or Hong Kong except what they make you learn in school. And I am not, not, not Chinese!

She turned to Rita now and told her, "I haven't the vaguest idea how to say that. If you want to know, why don't you go ask Tommy Choi? His mother and grandmother don't speak anything but Chinese."

"Yeah," said Rita. "But I bet his mommy never taught him how to say go blow it out your ear. That guy is so straight he wears grey flannel pants and a white shirt to school half the time."

"That's because he has a job right after school," Chloe said. Tommy was okay. He'd lived in Canada since he was a little kid and spoke English and French fluently. He wasn't weird, like Philomen. "Is he still there?" she asked.

Rita looked, then nodded. "Yeah. He's still there. Come on, Chloe. Let's get out of here, okay? I gotta meet Den."

"Yeah. And I gotta get home." It wasn't true. She didn't even want to go home and listen to Brynn carp and Phoebe whine. But she did want to get out of the schoolyard, away from that dumb guy and his dumb staring.

chapter 2

"So?" Edie said.

"So, what?" Brynn said. She had been dreading the question ever since she had caught up with Edie.

"So, what did that worm Evan want? Did he ask you to tell me something? Does the slug want to beg for forgiveness?" Edie's mouth was twisted into a bitter snarl. It was hard to believe that a few short weeks ago she had been so head over heels in love with Evan that she had covered all of her notebooks with his name.

"No," Brynn said. "Nothing like that."

Edie looked disappointed. "He didn't give you any message for me?" Brynn shook her head. "Then what did he want?"

"Nothing," Brynn said.

"But he said something to you."

"It was nothing important, Edie."

Edie's eyes narrowed. "If it's nothing, why won't you tell me? He's not making a play for you now, is he?"

The colour rose on Brynn's cheeks. "Don't be ridiculous," she said. "I'm not interested in Evan."

"Then you're the only girl in this whole school who isn't," Edie said. "Ever since I dumped him, every girl in Earl Barron has been drooling. It's disgusting."

Brynn shrugged. She knew that what Edie said was true. Girls were attracted to Evan not only for his good looks, but also for his easygoing nature. Brynn had always liked him.

"You're not going out with him any more," Brynn said. "What do you expect them to do?"

"I wonder if he's asked anyone to the dance yet," Edie said.

"Why do you even care?"

"I don't." But her voice had that familiar tremble in it. She was going to cry again, Brynn just knew it. Ever since Edie had told Evan to get out of her life, she had spent half her time cursing him and the other half moaning over him. Brynn didn't understand her.

"If you still like him," she said, "why don't you go and talk to him? Why don't you make up?"

"Make up?" Edie said, angry again. "Make up with that two-timing piece of slime? You have to be kidding. After what he did to me? I'm already the laughingstock of the whole school. What would people think if I took him back?"

"If you love him, what do you care what people think?"

"I never want to speak to him again," Edie said. Then she said, "Did he at least ask about me?"

Brynn studied her friend for a moment, then sighed. She had known Edie ever since they were in the second grade, and they had always been close friends. It wouldn't be right to start lying to her now. "Promise me you won't get mad," she said.

"Mad about what?"

"He asked me to the dance."

"He *what?*"

"He asked me to the dance. But I told him no."

"He asked you to the dance?"

"Edie, I told him I didn't want to go. I turned him down, okay? So take it easy."

"I don't believe it," Edie said. "First I find him sitting up at the lake with his arm around Suzanne Leguillette. And now he asks my very best friend to the spring dance."

Brynn sighed. If people didn't want answers, they shouldn't ask questions.

"Edie, if you feel so strongly about it, that just proves you're still in love with him. And if you're still in love with him — "

"Me, in love with that two-timing, two-faced, cheating, no-good . . ." She spluttered as she ran out of names to call Evan. "No way. I don't ever want to hear his name mentioned in my presence again, do you understand, Brynn?"

"Sure," Brynn said. "Whatever you say."

* * *

St. Urbain Street between Laurier and St. Joseph was one long line of three-story row houses. On each floor was a separate apartment. All the houses had doors at street level, hidden away behind a tangle of black wrought-iron staircases that wound their way up to the second floor, and then turned and twisted up to the third.

Phoebe hated those miserable stairs in the winter, when the ice clung to the iron. A person could kill herself shooting headfirst down two long flights and landing, splat, on the cement sidewalk. It figured they had to live on the third floor. There were three doorbells, one above the other, at the bottom of the stairs. Three strips of wood, painted white and hand-lettered in neat black letters, sat over the top bell. Laurendeau, read the first. Yan, the second. Then, Torrence. A lot of people couldn't figure out the bells. Was the top bell for the top floor? Or was the top bell really the first bell, the one for the first floor? And of course everybody thought that each of the three names belonged to a different bell, that Laurendeau lived on the first floor or the top floor, depending on how you looked at it. Yan was always in the middle, but Torrence could be either top or bottom. The bell-ringing drove the people on the bottom and middle floors crazy.

Laurendeau, Yan and Torrence all lived on the top floor.

As Phoebe rounded the corner, wondering if her sisters were already home, she saw a blue and white police cruiser sitting at the curb in front of her building. She looked around, and spotted a uniformed officer and a plain-clothes cop way up on the third-floor landing. They were knocking on her door.

It was finally happening, she thought. Just like her mother always said it would. The cops were coming to take Chloe away. Phoebe kept watching them as she approached the bottom of the stairs.

After a moment, the two cops turned and came back down. The younger one, the one in the uniform, brushed right by her. He didn't even glance her way. He was one of those cops, Phoebe decided, who treated kids like they were invisible. But the older one, a big man in a black suit, smiled at her from under his bristly black moustache.

"I don't suppose you live around here, do you?" he asked. His voice was booming, but friendly. His dark eyes twinkled. Phoebe nodded.

The big cop glanced up to the third-floor apartment. "You know Sheila Torrence, the woman who lives up there?"

The blood drained slowly from Phoebe's face. It wasn't Chloe they were looking for.

The big cop studied her a moment. "She wouldn't be your mother, would she?"

Phoebe stared up into his friendly dark eyes and tried to decide what to say.

* * *

"Mom's going to be royally ticked off, Chloe," Brynn said. "You know how her boss gets on her case whenever she has to take time off — because of you. If she gets fired on account of this . . . " Brynn scowled at her sister. "Why does Rusnek want to see her, anyway? What did you do this time?"

"I didn't do anything," said Chloe.

"Right. Sure. Rusnek just hauled you down to the office for no reason, right?"

"Noseworthy sent me."

"Come on, Chloe. What was it this time?"

"Nothing. Noseworthy doesn't like me. He's out to get me."

Brynn shook her head. Boy, Chloe just never quit. If you found her standing over a body, holding a knife dripping blood, she'd deny everything. *Murder? What murder?* "Tell me, Chloe."

"He just sent me down to the office, that's all. I didn't do anything."

"Does that *anything* you didn't do include your homework?"

"So what if it does? Who cares?"

"Mom's gonna care."

"Big deal. You're gonna tell me she was the Homework Queen of Earl Barron in her day? Get real, Brynn. There's a reason she's a waitress, you know. And scholarship isn't it."

Just the mention of their mother these days made Chloe angry. It was almost as if she hated her, but whenever Brynn pressed her for an explanation, Chloe either made a smart remark or walked away from the conversation.

"What's the matter with you?" Brynn said. "You think it's some big joke if Mom loses this job?"

It wasn't a job that required superior intelligence, and it didn't exactly keep them all in the style to which Brynn wished she were accustomed, but it was the best job their mother had ever had. Cocktail waitressing at the Uptown meant long hours but good tips. It brought in more money than the factory jobs that someone with their mother's education could expect. She had dropped out of high school at seventeen to marry Brynn's father, Yves Laurendeau. Four years later, he was killed in an accident, leaving Sheila on her own with a six-week-old daughter, no education, no job experience, and no real skills. She hadn't exactly had an easy time of it since then. There was no way Brynn was going to let Chloe spoil things for her now.

"Did you ever stop to think who'd dish out your allowance if Mom lost her job? We'd be on welfare."

"Will you relax?" Chloe said impatiently. "Geez, if it means that much to you, I'll suck up to Noseworthy. I'll do some homework this weekend."

As they came around the corner, Brynn saw the blue and white police cruiser sitting outside their place, and the big man in the dark suit talking to Phoebe.

"Great," Brynn said. "Now you're really in trouble."

"Me?" Chloe made a sour face. "The guy's talking to The Blob, for Pete's sake."

"Yeah. He's probably asking her for your whereabouts."

"Thanks a lot," Chloe said. "It's always nice to know your family is behind you one hundred percent."

Brynn said nothing as she hurried over to Phoebe. Her little sister's small eyes flooded with relief when she saw her. "He's looking for Mom," she said.

Sometimes being tall had its advantages. Brynn pulled back her shoulders, drew herself up to her full height and met the big plain-clothes cop's gaze with cool green eyes.

"What do you want with our mother?" she said.

"It's a police matter," the cop said. "Who are you?"

"Am I under arrest?"

The big cop looked puzzled.

"No," he said.

"Then I don't have to answer any questions."

"Wrong," Chloe said, coming up beside Brynn. "If a cop asks you, you have to identify yourself. Otherwise they can charge you with obstructing a police investigation or something like that."

"How do you know?" Brynn said.

Chloe rolled her eyes.

"Dumb question," Phoebe muttered.

Chloe ignored the comment. She was staring intently up at the big cop. "I've seen your picture in the paper," she said. "You're that homicide cop, right? The one who was on that big case last summer. You caught the guy who killed all those college students, didn't you?"

The big cop nodded.

"Levesque, right? Your name is Levesque?"

The cop nodded again. "And you are . . . ?"

"Chloe. And the big string bean is my sister, Brynn."

Most people did one of two things when they heard Chloe and Brynn were sisters. Either they assumed it was a big joke and started to laugh. Or they did a double take before making up their minds not to believe it. Levesque did neither.

"And your relation to Miss Torrence here is . . . ?"

"She's our sister, too." Chloe said. "What'd Mom do?"

"I didn't say she did anything."

"Then why are you looking for her?"

"I just want to ask her a few questions."

"About?"

Levesque smiled indulgently. "It's a police matter," he said. He dug into his jacket pocket and produced a business card. "Give this to your mother when she gets home. Ask her to give me a call, okay?"

Chloe reached for the card, but Brynn snatched it from his hand first.

"I'll see that she gets it," Brynn said. She always acted as if she was the only one capable of being responsible.

"I'd appreciate it," Levesque said. He turned and walked back to the cruiser.

"So," Chloe said as the car pulled away from the curb, "what do you think she did?"

"Mom? Nothing." Brynn said, but she was studying the card. She looked worried.

"The cops don't go looking for people who do nothing," Chloe said. "Hey, maybe she's an axe murderer and we don't know anything about it."

Brynn made a sour face. "It's your turn to make supper," she said.

"I've got plans," Chloe said. "I'm going out."

"Tough."

"Why should I make supper if I'm not going to eat it?"

"That's not my problem," Brynn said. "You know the rules. Everyone takes a turn making supper, everyone takes a turn cleaning up."

"Everyone except Mom," Chloe said. Their mother was usually either too tired from being on her feet all day — though never too tired, Chloe noticed, to do a quick change after a long bath and go out dancing all night with yet another man she had met at work — or she was working the night shift and wasn't home at all.

"If you don't make supper, I'll tell," Brynn said. "And Mom's going to be angry enough about Rusnek."

As Brynn preceded her up the stairs, Chloe stuck her tongue out. She wanted supper? Okay, Chloe would give her a supper she wouldn't forget.

chapter 3

When the phone rang, Chloe and Brynn both ran for it, Chloe from her room, where she was getting ready to go out, and Brynn from the kitchen where she and Phoebe had been eating supper.

"I'll get it," Brynn said. "You can do the dishes."

"But I made supper."

"Anything that comes out of a box and tastes that bad doesn't deserve to be called supper," Brynn said. "And anyway, I did the dishes for you twice already this week. You do the dishes. I'll get the phone."

Chloe made a face as Brynn picked up the receiver.

"Hello? Oh, hi, Mom."

Her mother's voice was quickly drowned out by the clatter of pots and pans.

"Mom, hold on a minute, okay?" Brynn held her hand over the receiver. "Will you shut up in there, Chloe? I can't hear."

There was one more resounding bang, then silence.

"What were you saying, Mom?"

"I have to work late tonight," her mother said. "I'm doing a shift for Yvette."

"Why? Is she sick?"

"No. But she's very upset. You remember Jean-

Luc, don't you, honey? He took me up to the Laurentians that time."

Brynn remembered. Her mother had gone out with him a few times the previous winter. He always wore silk shirts and a lot of gold jewellery.

"What's wrong with him?" Brynn asked. Nothing trivial, I hope, she thought to herself. He was one of the more unpleasant of her mother's male friends.

"He's dead," her mother said.

Brynn felt guilty for what she had been thinking. "Dead?" she said. "What happened?"

"Someone shot him." Her mother sounded rather calm about the situation. "Yvette needs some time off. She and Jean-Luc were planning to get married, you know."

Brynn hadn't known.

"Be a good girl, honey, and I'll see you later."

"Mom?" Brynn shouted before her mother could hang up. Quickly she told her mother about the police detective who had come to see her, and read her his phone number. She sighed when she finally set down the receiver. Another night without her mother. It seemed as if she was never home any more.

"Don't tell me," Chloe said when Brynn went back into the kitchen. "She has a hot date and won't be home till late."

"Geez, Chloe," Brynn said, annoyed.

Phoebe looked up from her plate. "Did you tell her a cop was here looking for her?"

Brynn nodded.

"Did she know what he wanted?" Chloe said. She

was squatting in front of the toaster, applying a layer of lipstick. She didn't even glance at Brynn.

"Remember that guy Jean-Luc? Well, someone shot him. She figures the cops want to talk to her about it because she knew him."

"Jean-Luc? The guy with no neck, looks like a gorilla?"

"Chloe, the man's dead. Can't you show a little respect?"

"Respect? For that guy?" Chloe shook her head in disgust. "I bet he had a record." She slipped the lid back onto the tube of lipstick and straightened up.

"Is there any more casserole?" Phoebe asked.

Brynn turned to stare at her. "You actually like that slop?"

"I'm hungry," Phoebe said.

"It's chemical garbage. It comes out of the box looking like wood shavings. If you stuck it on a shelf and let it sit there for the rest of the century, it wouldn't rot. It's preservatives held together with glue."

"It's convenience food," Chloe said, her voice like honey. "And that was real tuna in there."

"I thought it was good," Phoebe said, her eyes wide with hope. "So, is there any more?"

"You bet," Chloe said. She yanked the fridge door open and gestured with a flourish to the casserole dish on the top shelf. "I gotta run."

"Where are you going?" Brynn asked.

"Out."

"Out where?"

"Why? Who wants to know?"

"Mom does, for one."

"Right," Chloe said. "Did she tell you that when you were talking to her? Did she ask?"

"No, but . . ."

"I'll see you when I see you," Chloe said. She grabbed her red sweater off the hook by the door and strode out of the kitchen.

"Don't get into any trouble," Brynn called after her. "And it's a school night, so you better make sure you're back here before Mom or this time you're going to make her mad. I mean it, Chloe."

* * *

Chloe stepped out onto the landing and swung the front door shut behind her. It was like flicking a switch. One minute Brynn's high-pitched voice was ringing in her ears and the next minute she was surrounded by silence.

Get into trouble — what a joke, she thought. Even if she did get into trouble, what could her mother do about it? She had given up grounding Chloe. She was never home in the evenings to make a grounding stick. All she ever did was scream at her — "Where were you until two in the morning, were you with a boy, don't you know how much trouble you can get into with boys?" Right, Chloe thought. If anyone would know, it was her mother. Maybe if I keep my nose in a book all the time and work hard, I can be just like Brynn and never have any fun at all. No thanks, Mother dear.

Chloe smiled as she ran down the two flights of

stairs. She slipped a thumb through one belt loop of her jeans and headed down the street, enjoying the tickle of her thick black hair against the smooth skin of her bare arms. In her other hand she carried a sweater for later, after the sun had gone down and the air began to cool a little, especially on the mountain.

That's where she wanted to end up tonight. Way up on the mountain with Shadd, just the two of them, looking out over the city and the lights. It would be like looking at Christmas in June. Except that Rita would be there, and Den, of course. And maybe some of the others, Johnny Ramis and Johnny Connor and Maryanne. That was the problem. There was always someone around. She never got to spend any time alone with Shadd.

He was so cute. And tall. A good head taller than Chloe. He was strong too. His biceps were hard and smooth. When she was around him, Chloe usually found herself longing to run her hands over his arms, to feel that hardness and the warmth. And he had black eyes, like her own. Black like the night and full of mystery. Sometimes when he looked at her, her knees went weak.

He didn't say much. He was quiet. Not shy, though. It was more like he was watching and listening. The rest of the guys always said that Shadd only spoke when he had something to say that was worth hearing. Well, maybe tonight he'd find something worth saying to her, and maybe it would be about the dance.

25

It was a warm evening. All the old men who lived in ground-floor apartments had dragged their kitchen chairs out onto the sidewalk, along with their cans of beer and their packs of cigarettes. Now they sat drinking and smoking and talking to each other, their eyes watering, practically drooling every time a pretty girl went by. Chloe put a swing into her hips and a wiggle in her walk. Give the old guys something to really look at, she thought to herself.

A couple of younger guys whistled. Chloe grinned. She wasn't like Brynn. Brynn didn't like being whistled at, not that it happened all that often. Brynn was too skinny, all one line, and too tall for a girl. She had a pretty enough face, but pretty faces weren't what guys whistled at.

Chloe swung on down to Mount Royal and scanned the fringes of the park on the other side of the street. She didn't see any of her friends. She was early. She ran across the street and leaned up against the cool bark of one of the big oaks to wait and to think how she could steer Shadd around to the topic of the dance and make sure he got the idea that she wanted to go to the dance with him.

She glanced up the street. Oh, no! Geez, why did *he* have to show up? She ducked behind the oak and told herself maybe it would be all right. Maybe he hadn't spotted her. But there he was, staring right at her, his smiling face a short distance away from hers and closing fast.

"Hello, Chloe," he said in a soft voice. He sounded

so timid all the time. But he never hesitated to speak out in class, struggling through answers in his heavily accented English.

"Hiya, Philomen," she said. That was the other thing. His name. What kind of name was Philomen? It sure didn't sound Chinese. She thought maybe he'd chosen it for himself, given himself an English name so that he'd fit in. But, boy, any Canadian kid she knew who had a name like that would hate his parents forever for giving it to him. What a loser!

"You are waiting for someone?" he said, still smiling. He was always smiling.

"Yeah."

"Some friends?"

Chloe wondered if he smiled in his sleep. "Yeah."

"Chloe?"

"Yeah?"

"I want to ask you . . ." He was blushing. He cleared his throat and pulled himself up tall. "My friend Tommy Choi says that if my family had gone to Toronto or to Vancouver to live, things would be different because there are more Chinese people there. He says maybe that would make it easier for me. But my family is here. He says . . ."

Chloe rolled her eyes. Once Philomen got started, he didn't stop again in a hurry. He liked to talk. Let any teacher ask a question and not only would Philomen be the first to put his hand up, he'd wave it around over his head, like he was trying to flag down a cab on a rainy day. If the teacher called on

27

him, he'd jump to his feet and stand at attention beside his desk. Chloe had cracked up the first time he did it. The whole class had. But it hadn't fazed Philomen. Although his cheeks had turned red, he had stumbled through whatever he'd had to say, as if he couldn't hear the laughter all around him. The guy never gave up, which made Chloe want to scream. Because here he was standing right in front of her, not giving up.

She glanced around, then peered over his shoulder. Oh, no. Rita and Den were heading toward them. And right behind them was Shadd.

"Look, Phil, I gotta run, okay?"

"But, Chloe, I have not yet explained — "

"Practise your English on the trees, Phil," she said in a loud voice. Rita was closing in, and her ears would be all pricked up. "I really gotta run."

She didn't turn around to see the look on his face. Knowing him, he'd still be smiling. He probably hadn't even understood what she'd said. But she didn't care. That was his problem.

"Hey, Chloe, is this guy bothering you or what?" Den asked.

Den was Rita's boyfriend, although Chloe couldn't see what she saw in him. He made her feel uncomfortable. Half the time Chloe had the feeling that he wished Rita would drop her as a friend. The rest of the time, Chloe couldn't figure out what he thought. "No," Chloe said. "He's not bothering me."

"You sure?"

Den wasn't even looking at Chloe now. He was

staring at Philomen. Den was tall, even taller than Shadd. Philomen was a little guy, and slight. He smiled way up at Den and said, "Chloe and I were having a conversation."

Chloe's hands clenched at her sides. Who did he think he was, anyway, acting like they were friends?

"We weren't having a conversation," she said, glancing at Den and Rita and Shadd. Especially at Shadd. "He was the one doing all the talking. I don't even know what he was blabbering about."

"In other words," said Den, "he was bothering you, right?"

"Yeah, sort of. Who cares?"

What was wrong with everyone — always making a big deal out of things that were no big deal at all? Like Mr. Noseworthy and his stupid homework assignments, or like Brynn and whose turn it was to cook or to clean up. And now Den, like he even cared whether anyone bothered Chloe or not.

"Forget it, okay?" she said. "I thought we were going to get something to eat. I'm starving."

Den turned and looked at her. He had green eyes, like a cat's.

"Hey, Chloe, you don't want people to get the wrong idea about you, do you?" He said the words sweetly, as if he were really concerned. If a person ever needed proof that looks weren't everything, Chloe thought, they should get acquainted with Den Whitman. He had the good looks of a movie star, but the personality of an attack dog.

Chloe met his gaze. "You want to waste your time with that guy, it's okay by me," she said. She didn't want to hang around. She just wanted to get away from Philomen. "I'm hungry. I'm going to get something to eat." She felt Rita squirming around beside her, but resisted the urge to look at her. If she looked away from Den, he would think he had scored some points.

"Let's go, Den," Rita said. She tugged his arm. "I'm hungry, too. I haven't eaten all day."

Den glanced at Shadd, who was somewhere behind Chloe. Chloe kept her eyes on Den. In the end he shrugged, said, "Yeah, I guess you're right. This guy's a waste of time."

chapter 4

Phoebe rinsed a plate and set it into the dish drainer. Brynn picked it up and started drying it, glancing over at her mother, who had set up the ironing board in the middle of the kitchen. She was humming to herself as she stood in her bare feet, ironing an aquamarine dress.

"Where are you going tonight?" Brynn said.

"Out," her mother said.

Sometimes, Brynn thought, her mother sounded just like Chloe, which was funny, because just twenty minutes earlier, her mother had asked Chloe, "Where do you think you're going, young lady?" Chloe had answered exactly the way her mother had just now, and her mother had gone through the roof. Not that it had made any difference. Chloe had left the house without saying where she was going or with whom.

"Don't look so disapproving," her mother said now. "At my age, I can go out and have fun without having to report to my children." Brynn shook her head. It was strange that her mother and Chloe were so much at odds when they were so alike. Not in looks — her mother was tall and fair-skinned with hair that this year was flame red — but in temperament.

"Are you going out with someone?" Brynn asked.

"Yes, I'm going out with someone." But she

offered no details, and Brynn didn't feel up to coaxing them out of her. If her mother didn't want to tell her where she was going, that was her business. Brynn decided to broach another subject, one that she had been thinking about ever since the new sign had been hung from the schoolyard fence.

"They're offering night courses at Earl Barron starting in the fall," she said casually.

"That's nice," her mother said. She held up her dress and inspected it. Satisfied with her handiwork, she slipped the dress onto a hanger and turned off the iron.

Brynn screwed up her courage. "Maybe you should sign up for some classes, Mom." One of her mother's carefully shaped eyebrows arched.

"Why would I want to do that?"

Brynn pretended to concentrate on the glass she was drying. "You could finish high school. Get your diploma. Then, maybe later, you could take more courses and really get a good job." She thought maybe dental technician, or court reporter — they made good money. But the look on her mother's face silenced her before she could say any of it.

"I can't go to night school," she said. "I work nights."

"You could get another job. One that will leave your evenings free."

"I like the job I have now, thank you very much." She sounded offended. She folded the ironing board with a clank and shoved it into the cupboard. "Now if you don't mind, I have to get dressed." Brynn

32

watched as her mother padded out of the kitchen.

"I think you hurt her feelings," Phoebe said.

"I thought it was a good idea," Brynn said, picking up a dinner plate from the dish drainer.

Someone knocked at the front door.

"I'll get it," Phoebe said.

"No you won't," Brynn said. "I'll get it." She handed the plate back to her sister. "You keep washing. Only this time, make sure you get them clean." She grabbed a dishtowel from the rack and wiped her hands on it as she hurried through the living room calling, "Yeah, yeah, I'm coming."

She froze as she opened the inner door. The outer door was an enormous sheet of glass set in a heavy oak frame. She looked through it and saw Evan O'Neill standing out on the landing, his hands jammed into his jeans pockets.

"Evan," she said. "What are you doing here?"

"It's Friday night. I thought maybe you'd like to catch a movie."

Brynn shook her head. "I have to look after my kid sister."

"You do not," Phoebe said indignantly behind her.

Brynn turned and scowled at her. "I thought you were doing the dishes."

"No sweat," Evan said. "She can come with us."

"Oh, boy," Phoebe said. "What movie are we going to see?"

"What movie do you want to see?" Evan asked.

"We aren't going to see any movie," Brynn said.

"Awww . . . " moaned Phoebe.

"Come on," Evan said. "What else are you going to do on a Friday night?"

"I have to study."

"You can study tomorrow."

"I have to study tonight. Exams are only a few weeks away."

"Please, Brynn?" Phoebe said. "Let's go to the movies. It'll be fun."

"No," Brynn said. "Sorry, Evan." She hoped her tone made it clear that she wasn't sorry at all. "Now if you'll excuse me, I really have to study . . . "

Evan stood motionless a moment, staring at her so intently that she was afraid he was going to refuse to leave. But finally he shrugged and said, "Okay. But I'm warning you. I don't give up that easily."

Neither do I, Brynn thought. She closed the door and then turned and saw her mother behind her.

"That was a nice-looking boy," she said. "What did he want?"

"Nothing," Brynn answered. "Nothing at all."

* * *

They met at the burger place, Shadd and Den, Rita, the two Johnnys and Chloe. They all squeezed into a back booth for burgers with fries and gravy.

Chloe had been trying to stick as close to Shadd as possible, but when Shadd slid into one side of the booth, one of the Johnnys ducked in after him. That left Chloe stuck on the outside, a whole Johnny away from him. She scowled at the Johnny next to her; he grinned back at her.

"No good, man," Shadd said finally.

"What?" the Johnny said.

"We gotta switch seats. I'm too far away from my girl." Chloe beamed with pleasure as she slid off the vinyl seat to let Johnny out. Then she slid back in, nestling close to Shadd. This was going to be the night, she could feel it. Everything was going to work out just the way she planned.

"Hey, you want to shoot some pool?" the other Johnny asked after they had eaten.

Den pulled a pack of plain-tips from his pocket and lit one.

"Maybe," he said, blowing a cloud of smoke across the table at Chloe.

Chloe waved the smoke away angrily. She hated the smell of it. It made her eyes sting and her hair smell. It also annoyed her that Den insisted on smoking in front of Rita, when Rita was allergic to smoke. It made her eyes water and before Den even half finished his first cigarette she was always sniffling and sneezing. Too much exposure made her throw up. The only good thing about smoking was that maybe it would cut a few years off Den's life.

"What d'ya think, Shadd?" Den said. "You up for some pool?"

Shadd shrugged. He was leaning back in the booth, one arm draped over Chloe's shoulders. Chloe's entire being was focussed in on that arm. Her whole body tingled from its touch.

"I don't know," he said. "Maybe."

Disappointment washed over Chloe. Den didn't like to play pool with girls. Den didn't like to do anything with girls, except make out. An evening of pool meant an evening of hanging around some smoke-filled basement dive, watching Den and Shadd and the two Johnnys rack 'em up and shoot. She wouldn't have any time alone with Shadd.

"Hey, you guys," Rita said in a whiny voice. "All you ever want to do is shoot pool." Den glared at her.

"Yeah. So?"

"So," Rita said, "it's no fun. Why can't we do something else?"

"Like?" He gave the word a nasty spin so that it wasn't just a question any more, it was a challenge. Rita didn't stand up well to Den's challenges. She looked down at the tabletop, her shoulders slumped.

"Well, I don't know," she said. "Something fun."

"Pool's fun," Den said.

"How about taking a walk on the mountain?" Chloe said.

Rita looked up at her gratefully. Den made a face.

"A walk on the mountain?" he said, his voice high-pitched like a girl's. "What a lovely idea. Let's all take a walk on the mountain. Maybe we can watch some birds or pick some flowers."

Chloe glanced at Rita, who focussed on the Formica tabletop again.

"I don't know," said Shadd. "It doesn't sound like such a bad idea to me. We can find a nice quiet place to sit down, enjoy nature, you know what I mean?" He winked at Den.

But Den wanted to play pool and, as usual, what Den wanted, Den got. Chloe sat on a hard-backed chair to one side of the pool hall, her arms crossed over her chest, watched Shadd and the two Johnnys pick their cues while Den racked the balls.

"Would it kill him to take a suggestion from someone else just once?" she said to Rita. "Or does he always have to be the one calling all the shots? Geez, I don't know how you can stand it. He's so self-centred."

"He's nice to me," Rita said, but she sounded defensive.

"So I've noticed. He's so nice to you he lets you sit on the sidelines all night and watch. He's so nice to you he ignores you while he plays with his friends. He's so nice — "

"I like him," Rita said quietly. "If you were really my friend, you wouldn't be so negative about him."

"I *am* your friend," Chloe said, "which is why I can't stand it when you let a jerk like Den walk all over you."

"He does not walk all over me," Rita said indignantly.

"How come he never lets you play pool?"

"He says guys like to play pool with guys."

"Some guys like to play pool with girls, too, Rita. And how come he makes you sit in a smoky pool hall when he knows you're allergic to smoke? Doesn't he know you're going to be puking your guts up in another couple of hours?"

"It's not Den's fault this place is smoky."

"And I suppose it's not his fault that he smokes, either."

Rita stiffened. "He's tried to quit."

Chloe shook her head in disgust. "You're pathetic. If the guy was an axe murderer, you'd probably defend him. You'd be going around telling the whole world how it wasn't his fault."

Rita jumped to her feet. "That's not true!" She spoke so loudly that Den missed his shot and turned to scowl at her. "That's not true," she hissed again at Chloe. Then she strode across the room to find a chair closer to Den.

Chloe stood up and tied her sweater around her waist. What was the point of hanging around any longer? Den would have Shadd playing pool all night. She walked past Den's table without looking at him or Shadd or either of the Johnnys. She especially didn't look at Rita.

The evening air outside was cool and sweet compared to the stale, smoky atmosphere in the pool hall. Chloe sucked in a deep lungful before starting down the street. She had gone only half a block when she heard someone call her name.

"Wait up," Shadd said, loping toward her. "What's the matter? Where are you going?"

"Home," Chloe said. "I'm bored."

"You don't like pool?"

"Sure, I do. But when Den's around, I never get a chance to play."

Shadd laughed. "According to Den, it's a man's game."

"Yeah?" Chloe said. "Is that some kind of law? Or is it genetic? The ability to play pool is a characteristic associated with the Y chromosome?" Shadd laughed again, but there was a funny look in his eyes, like maybe he agreed with Den. That look threw Chloe. She liked Shadd. She didn't want him to be anything like Den.

"Hey, you want to do something, just you and me?" Shadd said. He stood close to her, so that she had to tilt her head back a little to look him in the eyes.

"Like what?"

"I don't know. Like take a walk on the mountain?"

Just the two of them? It was what she had been hoping for all night. She smiled and nodded.

* * *

Phoebe's stomach growled. It had been three hours since supper. Three boring hours with nothing to do but flip through the channels on TV.

"I wish you would have let Evan take us to the movies," she said. She could almost smell the hot buttered popcorn.

Brynn was folded into the leather chair in the far corner of the living room, a pool of light from the floor lamp behind her falling over the pages of her history text. She had pulled out her stack of books hours ago, right after Evan had left, and had scarcely looked up from them since. Phoebe shook her head. No wonder Chloe teased Brynn all the time about being a bookworm. Chloe would never have passed up a date with a cute guy like Evan, not even if she had an exam the next day.

Chloe reminded Phoebe a lot of their mother. They both liked to go out and have a good time. But whereas Chloe always seemed to do her best to make Phoebe feel terrible, her mother could always cheer her up.

Phoebe's stomach rumbled again. If only her mother were home more often. Ever since she'd taken the cocktail waitress job, it seemed that she was never around. With her out almost every night, the nights seemed so long and the apartment was so empty. As Phoebe listened to the noise her stomach was making, she wondered if she would ever be as popular as her mother or Chloe, or if she'd end up more like Brynn — stern, serious, businesslike.

Phoebe's stomach growled again, louder this time, so that Brynn, who was clear across the room, heard it. She frowned at Phoebe in annoyance.

"Geez, Phoebe. Stop it. I can't study with you making those disgusting noises."

"I can't help it," Phoebe said. "I'm hungry." In fact, she was ravenous. She thought with longing of the spare change she had scrounged from her mother's purse, and of the little corner store just across the street.

"Then get yourself something to eat."

"I can't. I'm on a diet."

Brynn rolled her eyes. "Sure. And I'm the Queen of England."

Tears stung the corners of Phoebe's eyes. She was used to Chloe talking to her like that, but it hurt when Brynn lost her patience and snapped at her.

"The prom is coming up," Phoebe said, "and I want to lose weight so I can go." Brynn said nothing. Phoebe wasn't even sure she had heard. She was looking down at her textbook again. "Brynn?"

"What?" Brynn said. She sounded angry and didn't even look up from her book.

"Nothing."

Brynn sighed and slammed her book shut. Then she reached up over her head and snapped off the light. "What?" she said, more gently this time. She got up out of the chair and came to sit on the couch beside Phoebe.

"Nothing. It's okay."

"Look, I'm sorry I yelled at you, Pheeb. But finals are coming up. I want to do well."

"You always do well." Phoebe said. She was tired of trailing through school in Brynn's wake. Teachers always commented on what an excellent student Brynn was and always seemed disappointed when Phoebe got only average marks.

"I want to do more than well."

Brynn's grim expression startled Phoebe. She seemed so determined. Then some of the stiffness went out of her and she gave Phoebe's arm a little squeeze. "So," she said, "what were you going to say?"

Phoebe chewed on her lip a moment. "How do . . . " she began, and then stopped. What if Brynn thought she was a loser?

"How do what, Pheeb?"

Phoebe searched her sister's eyes and then spit out all the words in one big breath. "How do boys decide which girls they're going to ask out? Is it just how they look, or is it something else? What do they want?"

Brynn stared at her for a moment and then, appallingly, she began to laugh.

Phoebe felt the blood burning her cheeks. "It's not funny, Brynn."

"Yes it is," Brynn said. "I've practically never had a date in my life and you're asking *me* what boys want? You should be asking Chloe."

"I know," Phoebe said. "But Chloe would just laugh at me. She doesn't like me."

"Sure she does," Brynn said. Phoebe wondered if Brynn really believed what she was saying. "Chloe's just going through a stage."

That was what their mother said every time Phoebe went crying to her about some humiliation Chloe had heaped on her, or some new torture she had devised. *Chloe's going through a stage.* It seemed to Phoebe that Chloe had been going through a stage all her life.

"I don't care about Chloe," Phoebe said. It wasn't true, but what was the point in talking about it? "I just want to go to the prom once in my life."

"Maybe next year," Brynn said.

42

Phoebe stared at her sister. "Next year? You're just like Cindy. She doesn't think I have a chance of being asked this year. Well, I'm going to show her. I'm going to show you. I'm going to go to that dance if it kills me."

Brynn tried to squeeze her arm again, but Phoebe yanked it free. Brynn shrugged and went back to her books.

chapter 5

The next morning, Brynn sauntered into the kitchen humming. Chloe glowered at her. If there was one thing she hated, it was putting up with cheerful people before she'd finished her first cup of coffee.

Brynn grabbed a clean mug from the dish drainer, poured herself some coffee from the pot on the back of the stove, and stirred in her standard three heaping teaspoons of sugar. Chloe didn't know how she could stand to take her coffee that way — it must taste like caffeine-laced syrup.

"So, how was the big date with what's-his-name?" Brynn said. She sounded as perky as a preschool teacher.

"None of your business," Chloe said.

"Ah," said Brynn. "Do I detect trouble in paradise? Did you two have an argument? Maybe break up?"

"Why don't you go play in traffic?" Chloe said.

"Hmm," Brynn said, studying her sister while she gulped down a mouthful of coffee. "If I had to choose, I'd say *break up*."

"We did not break up."

"You're in a lousy mood for someone who had a perfect night with the guy of her dreams."

"If I'm in a lousy mood, it's because I don't like being given the third degree."

Brynn took a loaf of bread from the breadbox, pulled out two slices, and dropped them into the toaster. "Did he ask you to the dance?" she said as she pushed the lever down.

Chloe stared stonily at her.

"He *didn't* ask you to the dance?"

Brynn couldn't believe it. Chloe had been talking about Shadd for weeks. When she talked that much about a boy, it meant she was interested in him, and, usually, whoever Chloe was interested in, she got.

"No, he didn't," Chloe said. "So what?"

"Is he going with someone else?"

"No." How was this even any of her business?

"So how come he didn't ask you?"

"He says he hasn't made any plans for the dance yet. He says he isn't sure he even wants to go."

Brynn's eyebrows crept slightly up her forehead. Chloe knew what she was thinking. Shadd Meadowcroft was one of the most popular boys in school. Girls of all ages lined the entrance to the locker room after football practice to tell Shadd what a great game he'd played.

"Maybe that's just a nice way of telling you that he doesn't want to go with you," Brynn said gently. "If I were you . . . "

"You're not me," Chloe said. "And I just finished telling you that it's not because he's taking someone else. He just isn't sure that he wants to go to the dance at all. He says he's getting bored with the same old stuff all the time. And for your information, I'll be seeing him tonight."

"Well, excuse me," Brynn said.

Her toast popped up golden brown and she slathered it with butter. Then she carried it and her mug of coffee out of the kitchen. Chloe listened to her footsteps fading down the hallway, and the gentle *fwoop* of her bedroom door closing behind her. She stared down into her own half-empty cup of coffee.

* * *

Phoebe awoke with a growling stomach to the scent of freshly toasted bread. It made her mouth water, and for a few moments she contemplated buttered toast topped with a layer of gooey melting peanut butter. Then she threw the sheet off her bed and swung her legs over the side. Her white thighs spread like lumps of dough on the mattress. It wasn't fair. Brynn's legs were long and skinny like a stork's. She looked great in jeans or a short skirt. Chloe's legs were much shorter — Chloe was a small person — but she was tiny all over. Phoebe doubted you could find much fat on her anywhere.

And then there was Phoebe. Chunky, baby-fat Phoebe with dimples on her elbows and dimples on her knees and even, although she would never admit it to anyone, dimples on her bum. Plump Phoebe with a rounded belly and thighs that rubbed together when she walked. Stout little Phoebe who had never worn a short skirt or one of those tiny T-shirts, even though everyone was wearing them now. It wasn't fair.

She stood up and pulled on a pair of baggy cords and a T-shirt that hung down to mid-thigh. She thought of it as her camouflage outfit. As she raked a brush through her blond curls, she steadfastly refused to pay attention to the delicious aromas emanating from the kitchen. This time she was going to go all the way. This time she wasn't going to cave in. This time she was going to win the battle of the bulge. She grabbed her purse from her desk and headed down the hall, past the closed door to her mother's room, past the door to Brynn's. She knocked and waited for Brynn to answer before pushing open the door.

Brynn was stretched out on her bed, munching on toast while she pored over another textbook. She glanced up at Phoebe.

"I'm going shopping," Phoebe said. "Can you tell Mom when she gets up?"

"Who are you going with?"

"Cindy." It was a lie, but not an important one. Phoebe, at thirteen, was old enough to walk downtown and shop by herself when she wanted to.

"When are you coming back?"

Phoebe groaned. "You sound just like Mom."

"That's because when she wakes up, she's going to ask me where you are, who you're with and when you're coming back. And if I don't know, I'm the one who's going to get yelled at."

Phoebe sighed. Because Brynn was the oldest, their mother relied on her to keep track of everyone.

"I'll be back in a couple of hours," Phoebe said.

The morning air was already warm when she shut the front door behind her. Birds chirped on the telephone wires, and from where she stood on the third-floor landing, she could see the deep green of Mount Royal rising majestically from the middle of the city. As she started down the iron staircase, she felt in her purse for some bus tickets. Then she had a thought. It was thirty minutes to downtown on foot. She wondered how many calories a walk that long would use up. More than riding the bus, that was for sure. She adjusted the shoulder strap of her purse and began to march purposefully down the street. This is the first day of a brand new Phoebe Torrence, she told herself.

* * *

Chloe was on her second cup of coffee when she heard rapping on the front door. She didn't make any move to get up and answer it. Brynn's room was right across from the door. The kitchen was at the back of the long narrow apartment. Let Brynn answer it.

Whoever was out there rapped again, a little louder this time. Then Chloe heard the creak of Brynn's bedsprings and the *slap-slap* of her bare feet on the hardwood floor. The voices, after the door opened, were muffled. Then the door closed, and Chloe heard two sets of footsteps. One stopped almost immediately — Brynn, going back to her room. The other was coming toward Chloe. She wondered who it could be.

48

Rita's head appeared first. She poked it in through the kitchen door and smiled weakly at Chloe. Her lips were trembling as she said, "Hi."

Chloe stared evenly at her.

"Are you still mad at me?" Rita said.

"I thought you were the one who was mad," Chloe said. She carried her mug to the stove and poured herself a fresh cup of coffee, without offering any to Rita.

Rita hesitated at the door, then slipped into the kitchen.

"I was," she said.

Chloe added a splash of milk to her coffee. "But not now?"

Rita shook her head. "I went home and spent half the night throwing up. My mother says if Den doesn't stop smoking around me, she's not going to let me see him any more."

That would be no great loss, Chloe thought. But she kept her mouth shut.

"I know you don't like him," Rita said. "But that doesn't mean we can't still be friends, does it? I mean, we've known each other practically forever."

Chloe took a sip of her coffee. It had been standing on the warmer too long and was thick and bitter. She dumped it out into the sink, then emptied the pot and threw out the filter and grounds.

"I'm going to make a fresh pot," she said, glancing at Rita. "You want some?"

Rita started to smile. She looked relieved. She must really be sorry, Chloe thought.

"I'd love a cup," she said.

"How 'bout some toast?"

Rita's smile broadened. "You have any peanut butter?"

Chloe nodded and produced a jar from the cupboard above the sink.

"So," Rita said as she watched Chloe measure the ground coffee into the filter basket, "I noticed Shadd left the pool hall right after you last night. Did you two do anything?"

Chloe filled the coffee maker with water and set the pot onto the warming pad. "We went for a walk," she said.

"A walk?" Rita grinned. "Where'd you go? Up to the lookout?"

Chloe nodded.

"And?" Rita prodded.

"And what?"

"And . . . you know. Did he ask you to the dance?"

It was the only thing anyone seemed interested in. Did he ask you to the dance? Chloe shook her head.

"But we were going to go together," Rita said. "Me and Den, you and . . . " She paused. "I bet Johnny Ramis would ask you if he thought you were interested. But you better hurry up. Johnny Connor already has a date, and you know how Ramis hates to be beat out by Connor."

"You couldn't pay me enough to go to the dance with Johnny Ramis," Chloe said. "His hands sweat, and he smells like breath mints."

"It's better than the alternative. I mean, you don't really want to sit around here the night of the dance, do you? And after the dance, we were all going to — "

"I don't plan to sit around here. I plan to be at that dance. With Shadd."

"But you just said — "

"I just said he didn't ask me last night. But I'm going out with him tonight . . . "

Rita's eyes widened. "You are? How come you didn't tell me?"

"I'm telling you now."

"I mean how come I didn't know about it already? I mean, we always do everything together, the whole gang."

Chloe was getting tired of the whole gang, especially when it always included Den.

"I'm going out with Shadd, just him and me. And I bet you anything that by the time the evening is over, he'll have asked me to go to the dance. I already know what I'm going to wear. Wait till you see this dress, Rita."

"You going to buy it or make it?"

Chloe rolled her eyes. What a stupid question! Couldn't Rita get it through her head that not everyone had a dentist for a father? Not everyone could trot down to Sherbrooke Street and buy a new dress every time there was a dance at school. Thank God for sewing machines, she thought, and the dozens of hole-in-the-wall wholesale fabric outlets that dotted the textile district in the east end.

Chloe could make anything for just a fraction of what it would cost to buy it ready-made in the store.

"I'm going to make it," she said. "Want to see the pattern?"

"Sure," Rita said. There was something eating at her, something that Chloe could see but couldn't read. "But I still think it wouldn't hurt to let Johnny Ramis know, just in case things don't work out the way you expected . . . "

"Things are going to work out," Chloe said. "I can feel it." Just like she'd felt Shadd's hands on her skin last night, and the softness of his lips against hers.

* * *

Phoebe walked slowly down the aisle, pretending to be studying the various types and shades of hair colouring, but really looking out of the corner of her eye at the diet products. There were so many people in the drugstore. Phoebe didn't want them all to know that she was on a diet. She picked up a box of hair dye and read the label, waiting for people to move on so that she could decide in private which diet product she wanted to buy.

A hand fell onto her shoulder. Startled, Phoebe spun around and stared up at a stern, grey-haired woman. "Are you going to buy that?" the woman said. "Because if you aren't, put it down. I've been watching you. I always watch kids like you."

Phoebe blinked in confusion at the woman, trying to understand what she had done wrong.

"You kids, you think you can come in here and take whatever you want and it doesn't hurt anybody. Well, I have news for you. It hurts me. It hurts my family. This is my store and stealing from it is like stealing food from my family's mouth."

Phoebe put the package of hair colouring back onto the shelf and started to back away. When she was halfway down the aisle, she turned and fled. It took six whole blocks for her heart to stop pounding and the blood to drain from her face. She came to a stop in front of a store that sold chocolate. Her mouth watered as she peered through the glass at the almond bark and the maple walnut fudge and the slabs of milk chocolate. The sweet smells wafting through the open door urged her to go inside. But she resisted. She actually resisted. She was proud of herself. She was even proud of the angry grumbling sounds her stomach was making. She turned away from the shop window and peered up the street, looking for another drugstore.

When she found one, she marched straight to the aisle where the diet products were shelved and, although her cheeks felt hot, she openly scanned all the items. She settled at last on a product she had seen advertised in dozens of magazines. It came in a heavy little container that looked as if it contained chocolates. The picture on the lid showed a cup of steaming tea, with two little caramel-like squares nestling on the saucer next to it. Phoebe carried it to the cash, plunked it down along with her money, and gazed steadfastly out the window while the cashier rang up the sale. Then she carried the bag containing her purchase out of the store and walked to a downtown park. She stopped in at a little coffee shop across from the park and ordered a cup of tea in a styrofoam cup. She carried her tea to the park, settled herself on one end of a bench and pulled her box of SlimNow from its bag. She peeled off the cellophane wrapping and removed the lid.

Inside the box were row upon row of tiny waxed-paper-covered cubes. Phoebe selected two, just like the picture on the front of the box, and then slipped the box back into the bag. She unwrapped one of the cubes and popped it into her mouth. It tasted vaguely of caramel, with a sort of chalky aftertaste that she washed away with the hot tea.

She smiled to herself as the rumblings in her stomach subsided. She had done it, she thought. She had found the solution to all her problems. In a few weeks she would be as slim as Chloe, and then, for sure, someone would ask her to the dance.

chapter 6

"Will one of you get the door, please?" Sheila called. "I'm not dressed yet."

Brynn, who was polishing the coffee table, looked expectantly at Chloe. "Get that, will you?" she asked.

The knocking grew more insistent. Chloe didn't move.

"You get it," she said, as she unscrewed the top of a bottle of nail polish. "I'm busy."

"But you're closer."

The knocking grew louder.

"Girls!" Sheila called from her bedroom.

"Chloe!" Brynn said in exasperation.

"You could have been there by now," Chloe said as she swept the nail polish brush expertly over the toenail on her big toe. Brynn stormed past Chloe and marched down the hallway. She froze as soon as she opened the inner door. Standing on the landing was the plain-clothes cop who had been looking for her mother a week ago. He was wearing a black suit, but it wasn't the same as the last time she had seen him. This one was better cut. It had real style to it. He had a box of chocolates in one hand. Brynn knew the brand; they were expensive.

She struggled with the front door lock. It could be stubborn if you forgot you needed to twist it just so, and suddenly she didn't seem able to remember anything. By the time she finally got it open, her face was red and sweat had beaded on her temples.

"Le– " she began, then suddenly remembered she only knew that his name was Levesque. She didn't know his rank. You couldn't call a cop by just his last name. "Hello," she said instead.

"Hello." As he spoke, he looked past her, down the hall. "Is your mother here?"

"My mother?" What did he want her for now? More questions about Jean-Luc's death?

"I've come to pick her up," he said.

Brynn's knees buckled. Pick her up? Isn't that what cops said when they were going to make an arrest?

"We're going out to dinner," he added.

Brynn was certain she hadn't heard correctly. This big cop was here to pick up her mother for a date? It was just like her mother not to mention a word about it.

"She . . . she's not dressed yet."

He smiled. It took Brynn a moment before she remembered what she should do.

"Would you like to come in?" she asked. "To wait, I mean."

"Thank you very much," Levesque said. He carried the box of chocolates casually, as if it were a newspaper rolled and tucked under his arm.

"I'll tell her that you're here." But before she could take a step down the hall toward her mother's room, her mother called out, "I'll just be a minute. Have a seat, Louis."

Brynn waved toward the living room and he smiled again. "Chloe," Brynn said, following Levesque down the hall. "Chloe, we have company."

Chloe glanced at Louis Levesque as if a cop strolling into their living room were an everyday occurrence. "Still grilling Sheila for information?" she said. Brynn shook her head. Sometimes she thought her sister had no respect for anyone or anything.

"He's here to pick up Mom," Brynn said. Even Chloe couldn't meet that news with total indifference. Her nail polish brush slipped in her hand, and a blaze of scarlet danced over her toe. "He's taking her out to supper."

Chloe appraised Levesque carefully. "Are you married?" she said.

"Chloe!" Brynn said.

Levesque shook his head.

"Divorced?" Chloe said.

"Yes."

"A-ha!" Chloe smiled. "Kids?"

He shook his head. "No."

Chloe studied him again. "It's possible," she said.

Levesque smiled at Chloe in a way that gave Brynn a chill. He seemed to be looking right into her. "You mean, it's possible someone wants to take your mother out for dinner?" he said.

Chloe reached for a cotton ball and a bottle of polish remover. She dabbed carefully at the stain on her skin. Then she looked Levesque straight in the eye, and Brynn knew that it had been an illusion.

He hadn't seen into Chloe at all. He had just thought he had.

"I mean, it's possible you could end up being number four," Chloe said.

Levesque didn't get it. He fell right into Chloe's trap. "Number four what?" he said.

Chloe laughed. It was the kind of laugh you heard in cheesy midway fun houses.

"He doesn't know," she said to Brynn. "Do you think we ought to warn him? Or should we let him figure it out for himself? After all, he's a hotshot homicide cop. Detective Lieutenant Louis Levesque. Pride of the department."

Lieutenant! Finally Brynn knew what to call him. "Can I get you something to drink, lieutenant?" she said.

"No, thank you," he said.

"Maybe you'd like to read the newspaper while you wait." He declined the offer with a shake of his head. "I'm fine, thank you," he said. "I'm enjoying my conversation with your sister. And I'm curious about number four."

"Sheila eats men alive," Chloe said.

Brynn's ears pricked up at the sound of footsteps on the iron staircase outside. She heard the front door open, then close. As Phoebe came down the hall with a brown paper bag in one hand, Brynn went to meet her. "Where have you been?" she said. "You said you'd be home by noon. You were gone all day. And you weren't with Cindy. I checked. Mom was ready to call the police."

"I went for a walk," Phoebe said.

She was pale and her face seemed pinched as she brushed by Brynn. "Do we have any tea?"

"Tea? You don't drink tea."

"Yes I do," Phoebe said.

Brynn followed Phoebe down the hallway and almost slammed into her when she came to a sudden stop. Phoebe was staring at the big policeman in the living room.

"Lieutenant Levesque is here to take Mom out to supper," Brynn said.

Phoebe stared at her a moment, then looked to Chloe for confirmation.

Chloe just shrugged. "That's what he says. I've been trying to warn him about the last three guys that Sheila got serious with, but that doesn't seem to deter him. Maybe he wants to be our new daddy."

"I don't know if I could handle three daughters like you," Levesque said mildly.

"There aren't three like me," Chloe said. "I'm unique."

"Thank God," Brynn said.

Phoebe disappeared into the kitchen with her small parcel. Brynn sat down on the edge of the couch and smiled at Levesque while Chloe went back to painting her nails. The silence in the room was broken only a few minutes later when the kettle began to whistle in the kitchen.

"Are you making tea?" Chloe called.

"Yeah," came Phoebe's voice.

"Make me some too."

Brynn stared pointedly at Chloe. "Maybe the lieutenant would like some," she said.

Chloe stared right back at her. "So why don't you ask him? You're sitting right next to him."

Brynn felt like smacking her sister. She could be so rude. She turned to Levesque. "Would you like some tea?"

"No, thank you," Levesque said.

Phoebe appeared with two mugs of tea and handed one to Chloe.

Chloe peered at her. "What are you eating?" she said.

"Nothing," Phoebe said. But she looked flustered and Brynn was sure that she had been chewing something when she came into the room.

"Let me smell your breath," Chloe said.

"No!"

"Chloe, for Pete's sake — " began Brynn.

"You big blob, if you touched that last piece of cheesecake, I'll murder you," Chloe said. "That was mine. I only had one piece, not four, like you."

"I didn't touch your stupid cheesecake," Phoebe said. Her chin started to quiver. Tears welled up in her eyes.

"Leave her alone, Chloe," Brynn said. "Besides, I threw that cheesecake out last night."

"You *what?*"

"There was mold growing on it. Mom brought that cheesecake home over a week ago. What were you planning to do with it, Chloe? Enter it in the science fair?"

"I looked at that cheesecake yesterday morning and it was fine," Chloe said. "You're lying, Brynn. The Blob ate my cake and you're lying to cover up for her."

"Okay," Phoebe said. Tears rolled down her cheeks. "Okay, I ate your stupid cake. You weren't going to eat it. You never eat it. You just let it sit there until I eat it and then you scream at me."

"Are you happy now?" Brynn said. "You got what you wanted. She's crying."

"Because she's a crybaby as well as a blob."

"Chloe!"

"Well, it's true."

Phoebe turned and ran down the hall, mug in hand, steaming tea slopping out of it and onto the hardwood. *Slam* went her bedroom door.

Brynn glowered at Chloe and got up to go after Phoebe. Levesque stood quickly as Sheila swept into the living room in a little black dress. She looked stunning. She always did when she was going out.

"What's going on?" she said, annoyed, but trying not to show it in front of Levesque.

Chloe looked over the rim of her mug at Levesque. "Guess you're glad you don't have kids, eh?" she said.

* * *

Brynn sighed. If it isn't one thing, it's another, she thought. First Chloe makes a real idiot of herself trying to show Levesque what a hotshot she is. Then Phoebe starts blubbering over something

61

Chloe says. Anyone else would have figured Chloe out by now and would just duck when she started lobbing the grenades. Or they'd fight back. But not Phoebe. Then, after Sheila and Levesque had left, after Chloe had taken off for her date with Shadd, after Brynn had got Phoebe settled down again, there was Evan at the door. Brynn felt like screaming at him, "Don't you ever give up?" But that would have been too rude. It was something Chloe might have done. So instead, when Evan asked her if she'd like to take a walk, maybe buy some ice cream since the night was so warm, she said, "I can't. I have to study."

He seemed to find this amusing. "Again?"

"Always."

"You're already near the top of the class."

"I don't want to be near the top. I want to be at the top." Not only was she going to finish high school, unlike her mother, she was going to win a scholarship to university. She wasn't going to quit until she got exactly what she wanted, and no one was going to stand in her way.

Evan didn't laugh. He didn't look at her like she was crazy, either. "You sound pretty determined," he said.

"I am, Evan, so I really have to get back to work." She started to close the front door, but he was blocking it and he didn't step back. "Look, Evan . . . "

"Everyone needs a break now and then," he said. "Fifteen minutes, what do you say? We'll walk over to Park Avenue and I'll buy you an ice cream cone and then I'll walk you right back here so you can get back to your studying, I promise." He held his hand over his heart. "Fifteen little minutes. What could it hurt?"

"You promise you'll leave me alone if I say yes?"

"I swear I won't bother you again tonight."

It wasn't exactly what she'd had in mind, but still she found herself saying yes. Just this once, she told herself. And she could use a little break. She felt in her pocket to make sure she had her key before she followed him down the stairs to the street.

It was warm outside. The sun was still hanging in the sky above the crest of the mountain. She had been inside for so long, lost in her notebooks and her studying, that she had almost forgotten there were nights like this.

Evan walked along at her side, mercifully making no attempt to hold her hand. After they had gone one block in silence, he glanced over at her and said, "So how come you don't like me?"

She felt herself start to blush. "I never said I didn't like you."

He grinned. "So I guess it wasn't my imagination after all."

He let the words hang between them until she couldn't stand the suspense any longer. "What wasn't your imagination?"

"That time Jennifer was sick and you and I got to be lab partners. Boy, that was the best lab period I ever had. And the whole time we were dissecting that frog, I had the feeling that you weren't exactly having a terrible time. In fact — "

"I don't want to talk about this, Evan."

"But it's fate," he said. "Don't you get it? Jennifer getting sick that day was the best thing that ever happened to me."

"You were going out with Edie at the time."

"Edie and I are like the Romans. Ancient history."

"Two weeks ago sounds pretty recent to me. And Edie happens to be my best friend."

"Two weeks or two years, what's the difference? Edie and I aren't together anymore. I'm more interested in current events than I am in history. Come on, Brynn, say it. You like me."

They had reached the ice cream shop. Evan pushed open the door and stood aside the let her pass. She went inside, wishing she had stayed at home.

"What'll it be?" Evan said, walking along the counter and staring into the vats of ice cream behind the glass. "Rocky Road? Banana Split? Mocha Supreme? Pralines and Cream?"

"Vanilla," Brynn said. "One scoop, please." She had lost her taste for ice cream. All she wanted was to get back to her books, away from Evan.

"Make mine a double Rocky Road," Evan said.

They carried their cones back outside. "How about a walk on the mountain?" Evan said.

Brynn shook her head. "You said fifteen minutes. You didn't say anything about a walk. I have to get back to work."

"On a Saturday night?"

She gave him a sharp look.

He sighed. "Okay, okay. You can't blame a guy for trying. Come on, I'll walk you home."

As they turned back toward her neighbourhood, Brynn glanced across the street and saw Edie standing on the sidewalk, staring first at Brynn and then at Evan.

"Oh my God," Brynn said. She raised a hand to wave and called, "Edie! Edie, wait!"

But Edie had already turned and was running down the street. Brynn glowered at Evan. "Now look what you've done," she said.

chapter 7

"Why don't we go up the mountain?" said Chloe. It was the third time she had suggested it. Every time she did, Shadd gave a little nod. But Den always said no.

How had Den even ended up with them anyway? It wasn't what she had planned. It didn't seem to be what Shadd had planned either. One minute she had been strolling down St. Urbain, her hand caught in Shadd's, her red sweater hanging from her arm, and a great big satisfied smile on her face. The next minute a too-familiar voice called, "Hey, Shadd."

It was Den. With Rita.

"Hey, what a coincidence, us running into you like this, eh?"

Chloe glanced at Rita, who shrugged, as if it weren't her fault. But she didn't look Chloe in the eye. "Come on, Den," she said. "Let's go."

But Den wouldn't go. Not until Shadd agreed to go with him. It looked like they would never get to the mountain. First Den wanted to play a little pool. Then he wanted to find Johnny Connor because Johnny owed him some money. Now he had the money and he was looking for something else to do.

"The mountain," said Chloe.

"Yeah," said Rita. She was plastered up one side of Den, hooked in under his arm, doing her best to set things right. "Let's go up the mountain, over beside that lookout, you know, where there's all that soft grass and all those bushes."

Den grinned. He leaned down and planted a kiss on Rita's cheek. Great, thought Chloe. Finally she was going to get what she had been looking forward to all day. She was going back to the mountain with Shadd.

After he'd kissed Rita, Den said, "I got a better idea."

Chloe groaned. Shadd didn't say anything.

Rita said, "What better idea?"

"Let's go get some Chinese food."

"Chinese food?" Chloe couldn't believe it. "You just had a hamburger at the pool hall."

"That was nearly two hours ago."

Two hours? Chloe glanced at her watch. The night was speeding by. If they didn't go to the mountain soon, they'd never go.

"I know," said Rita. She sounded as bright and perky as Brynn always did first thing in the morning. It was just as irritating. "Let's go get some Chinese food and take it up to the mountain and have a picnic in the moonlight, under the stars." She squirmed around in her tight jeans as she spoke, and Den started to nod like he thought it was a pretty good idea. Chloe didn't care, as long as they ended up on the mountain.

"Okay," she said. "Let's go. There's a place at the end of the block that just opened up. We can get some stuff there."

"I know a place down on Lagauchetière," said Den. "Let's go there."

"Lagauchetière?" Chloe said. "It'll take us an hour to walk down there. There's a place right at the end of this block. You can see the sign from here."

"Yeah, but I know this place on Lagauchetière," said Den. "I know they serve good stuff. How do you know this new place is any good?"

Behind her, Shadd laughed. He slipped an arm around Chloe. Why couldn't they just go up to the mountain, *now*?

"Chloe's right, Den," said Shadd. "I don't know about you, but I don't want to spend an hour walking when I can spend that time up on the mountain with some good food and a pretty girl instead."

There was a God after all, thought Chloe, and he was smiling down on her right now. Den nodded, and together they made their way down to the end of the block. Shadd kept his arm around Chloe the whole way.

The front door of the restaurant was open when they got there, and Chloe's mouth began to water as she inhaled the aromas that spilled out into the night. She glanced at Rita, who smiled. "Well?" she said to Den. "What do you think?"

Den shrugged, but he led the way inside.

The place was small, with no more than a dozen tables, all crammed close together. At the back of the room was a long counter and behind that, a swinging double door into the kitchen. The place was empty except for an old man sitting on a chair behind the counter. He looked up at them when they came in. His leathery face split into a thousand wrinkles as he smiled.

"We want some takeout," said Den. "Egg rolls with some of that plum sauce, chop suey, pineapple chicken, fried rice, and, oh yeah, a double order of those little sweet and sour spareribs. And put a rush on it, will you, gramps? We don't have all night."

The old man's smile vanished. He frowned at Den. Chloe thought maybe the man hadn't understood what Den had said, he had spoken so quickly.

"Menu there," the old man said at last, and nodded to a couple of big blackboards mounted on the back wall alongside the doors to the kitchen. One of them was covered with Chinese characters, the other with block lettering in English. Hot and sour soup, egg drop soup, shrimp with lobster sauce, garlic beef with green peppers and snow peas, spring vegetables. Den studied it a moment and then said, "We don't want any of that stuff. We want egg rolls. Egg rolls and chop suey — "

"Not chop suey house," the old man said. He sounded really mad about it, like Den had insulted him.

"What are you talking about?" said Den. "This is a Chinese restaurant, isn't it? We want some Chinese food. To take out. Now."

"No chop suey," the old man said. He picked up a

spoon from behind the counter, a long metal spoon with a black plastic handle, and jabbed it at the menu on the wall. "No egg rolls. No chop suey. Menu there."

He kept waving the spoon around, and one swipe just about caught Den on the end of the nose. Den reached out and grabbed it and tried to wrench it away from the old man, but the man held on tight. Den looked surprised that the spoon hadn't just come away in his hand. He pulled a lot harder, but the old man not only held on, he shook Den loose. When Den cursed at him, the old man whacked him over the head with the spoon. Den yelped in pain and anger. Before anyone could stop him, he lashed out and punched the old man.

Chloe had never seen a real live person hit another real live person that hard. She'd always thought those sounds you heard in the movies were just made up. Now she knew it for sure. The real sound of one person hitting another person was much worse than anything she had ever seen in the movies.

The blow sent the old man reeling. Den still looked mad when he turned to them and said, "Let's get out of here." It was the first intelligent thing Den had said since Chloe had known him. She headed for the door. Behind her she heard Shadd yell, "Watch out!"

She turned around just in time to see Shadd lunge across the counter at the old man, who was coming forward waving the spoon menacingly over his head. Shadd shoved hard with both hands, and the old man staggered backward and then fell. There was a sickening crack when the back of his head hit and then bounced off the corner of a grill stove.

"Geez," Chloe said. She went close enough to the counter to look over and see the old man sprawled on the floor. "Maybe you killed him."

"Crazy old fart," Den said. "You'd have to shoot a guy like that to kill him." He went around the counter and bent to the crumpled old man. He was half sitting, half lying, his head lolling forward. Chloe saw the colour drain from Den's face. She watched him freeze. Then he looked at Shadd.

In slow motion, Shadd moved around behind the counter. He knelt down beside the old man, and stretched out a hand to touch his neck. Chloe had seen that done a million times in the movies. You feel the artery in the neck and you can tell if the guy has a pulse, you can tell if he's still alive. Shadd straightened up slowly.

"He's still breathing," he said. But he looked worried.

"We should call an ambulance or something," Chloe said. She looked around. There had to be a phone in here somewhere.

"Are you crazy?" Den said. "The next thing you know, the cops will turn up. You know what kind of trouble we'll be in then? That old man's going to say we attacked him. No one's going to believe he swung first."

He's an old man, Chloe thought. Den could have just walked away — well, he could have if he wasn't Den. And Shadd . . . She knew Shadd hadn't meant to push the guy that hard. She didn't want him to get into trouble.

"Someone's coming!" Rita said.

Den went into a crouch. "The back way," he said.

Chloe hesitated, but Rita grabbed her by the wrist, and before she knew it, Chloe was running too. Running out through the kitchen, running out into the alley, running out the other end and down another street, Rita's hand around her wrist, Shadd and Den thundering along ahead of them.

* * *

"Don't you want any ice cream?" Cindy asked.

Phoebe shook her head.

"How about a hamburger?"

"I'm not hungry," Phoebe said.

Cindy stared at her in astonishment. "We've been skating for nearly two hours. Usually that's more than enough to work up an appetite for a burger and fries. What's the matter with you? Aren't you feeling well?"

"I feel fine," Phoebe said. Why couldn't Cindy just take her word that she wasn't hungry? Why couldn't everyone stop paying so much attention to what she ate or didn't eat?

"Okay," Cindy said. "I was just asking. You don't have to bite my head off."

"I didn't bite your head off."

Cindy opened her mouth to say something then,

but suddenly broke into a grin and jabbed Phoebe in the ribs with her elbow. "Look," she whispered. "It's Bobby Keough. And he's coming this way. He's been looking at you all night, Phoebe. I think he likes you."

"That's not funny," Phoebe said.

Cindy looked surprised. "It wasn't meant to be." She straightened up, waved and called to him. "Hi, Bobby. What are you doing here?"

"Obviously," Phoebe said, "he's skating. What else do you do at a roller rink?"

Bobby Keough glided to a stop between them.

"Hi, Cindy," he said. Then he turned his clear blue eyes on Phoebe. "Hi, Phoebe."

"Hi, Bobby," Cindy said again. Then she giggled.

"So," said Bobby, blushing a little by now. "I was just going to get something to eat. Are you two hungry? You guys want anything? You want to join me?"

Cindy jabbed Phoebe in the ribs.

"No thank you, Bobby," Phoebe said. She was surprised at the disappointment in Bobby's eyes. "B . . . but maybe a diet soda," she said quickly. Cindy nudged her and winked at her. "I . . . I'm sort of on a diet." She surprised herself by telling him that, but it seemed important that he know, that he understand that she was doing something about her weight. Bobby's smile made her glow inside.

He looked at Cindy. "How about you? What'll you have?"

"The same."

Bobby nodded and rolled across the rink toward the refreshment stand.

"I told you," Cindy said. "I told you he was watching you."

Phoebe stared at him as he leaned on the counter and gave the girl behind it his order. Was it possible? Had Bobby Keough really been watching her?

"I wonder if he's asked anyone to the prom yet," Cindy said. "Want me to find out?"

"No," Phoebe said quickly.

"But don't you want to know? If he hasn't already asked someone, maybe he'll ask you."

She had been thinking — hoping — the same thing herself. But when she heard Cindy say it, it suddenly sounded ridiculous.

"He won't ask me," she said. "Nobody's going to ask me."

Cindy looked at her with surprise. "Why not?"

"You know," Phoebe said. She looked down at her round belly and her chubby thighs.

"No I don't," Cindy said. "What's wrong? Why wouldn't he ask you?"

Why was Cindy acting as if there wasn't a problem? Did she think it was funny?

"Because," Phoebe said, "I'm fat."

"You are not," Cindy said. But she didn't sound convinced of what she was saying.

"Yes I am. You've said so yourself. You said if I didn't stay away from pizza, nobody would ask me out."

"I didn't mean it," Cindy said. "Really. I don't even know why I said that."

"I have thighs that rub together, and cheeks like

74

a chipmunk. What do you call that? Skinny?"

"Not fat," Cindy said.

"What then?"

"What's the big deal anyway?" Cindy said. "So what if you're not a string bean? It doesn't matter — "

"Guys never ask out fat girls. They don't like fat girls. They only like skinny girls."

"But Phoebe — "

"Never mind. I don't want to talk about it."

Cindy lowered her voice. "He's coming back with our drinks."

Phoebe's pulse began to race. She wanted to run, but she still had on her roller skates and, besides, her knees felt wobbly. She accepted the can from Bobby. Cindy took hers, and they all sipped in silence a moment.

"So, Bobby," Cindy said slowly. "You have a date for the prom yet?"

Phoebe shot a sharp glance at Cindy, but Cindy simply refused to meet it.

Bobby's cheeks reddened. "I . . . I haven't . . . I mean, I didn't actually . . . "

Phoebe almost melted. Then, *whumpf*, something shot into Bobby from behind. "Hey!" he shouted as he lurched forward, stumbling into Phoebe, sending her into the boards. He pressed against her, and his face nuzzled into her neck just for a moment. It felt heavenly. Then he lost his footing and started to fall again. Phoebe grabbed him to keep him on his feet, and they scrambled and scuffled, but ended up together on the surface of the rink, helpless with laughter. Only then did Phoebe look up to see what had caused the mishap. Bobby Keough's little sister was standing with her hands on her hips.

"I've been looking for you for an hour," she said. "Dad's here. He's waiting."

Bobby struggled to his feet. "I gotta go," he said. His cheeks were flame red. Phoebe had never seen anything that colour that wasn't on fire.

"I told you," Cindy said after he had gone. "I told you he liked you."

Phoebe stared down at her can of soda. Maybe it was possible, she thought. Maybe somebody would ask her.

* * *

"I'm sorry, Brynn," Mrs. Hill said, "but Edie went to bed early. She said she was tired. Frankly, dear, she hasn't been feeling well since she and Evan broke up. But I'll be sure to tell her that you called."

"Thank you, Mrs. Hill," Brynn said. As she hung up the receiver, she felt sure that Edie would not return her call. In fact, it wouldn't have surprised her if Edie never phoned her again.

chapter 8

It was still dark when Chloe sat up in bed. She had never been up so early on a Sunday morning. She flipped her radio on and managed to catch two brief newscasts on two different stations. Neither of them mentioned the old man.

Maybe that was good. Surely if something really bad had happened, it would have been on the news. A man gets killed, people pay attention. But she wasn't satisfied until she retrieved the morning paper from the bottom of the stairs and crept back to her bed with it.

She scanned each page, top to bottom, even the little one-paragraph articles in the bottom corners next to the ads for computers. She almost missed it because it turned out to be a bigger article than she had expected. But there it was. She read the first few paragraphs three times, because at first she wasn't sure the article was the one she was looking for. Then she felt relieved. The old man was still alive. Shadd hadn't killed him.

Two boys, the article said, had come into the restaurant just in time to see several people fleeing out the back way. They didn't chase the people because they saw the old man lying behind the counter. The police said that apparently nothing had been stolen. The till was still full of cash. The police hadn't been able to question the old man yet, because he was unconscious. They did say that they had found an item of clothing in the restaurant that no one in the old man's family remembered seeing before. They said it was possible that this article of clothing could help them find the old man's assailants.

Article of clothing?

Chloe didn't remember seeing any article of clothing. But then, she hadn't really looked around the place. She had focussed first on the menu, and then on the old man. She was pretty sure, though, that whatever it was, it must have been there before they arrived. Shadd hadn't left any article of clothing there . . .

Then it hit her — her red sweater, the one she'd brought along in case it got cool!

She bolted off the bed, raced to her closet, threw open the door and pawed among the hangers and searched through the clutter on the floor. No sweater. She emptied her drawers, then ripped the sheets from her bed. Maybe she had dropped the sweater on her bed last night and it had gotten tangled in the sheets. But no. It wasn't in her bedroom. Nor was it in the living room, the bathroom, the kitchen or the hall closet. It wasn't anywhere. She clasped her head in her hands and rocked back and forth.

* * *

Brynn gathered up her warm clothes from the dryer and carried them to one of the tables at the back of the laundromat. What a way to spend Sunday morning. She and Phoebe and Chloe took turns doing everything — cooking, cleaning, doing the laundry. Of all the chores, laundry was the one Brynn hated the most. The way her mother was going, they'd never have enough money to buy their own washer and dryer, even the small apartment-sized ones. And the most exasperating part of it was that her mother didn't even seem to care. "There are more important things," she always said. "Besides, the laundromat is just around the corner."

Brynn opened a washing machine and pulled out another armful of clothes. They were damp and wadded together. She dropped them into a dryer and fed in some coins. Then she went back to the table and began to fold the dry clothes.

"Want some help fluffing and sorting?" said a voice behind her.

Brynn glanced over her shoulder. Not again! What was it with Evan? Why couldn't he just take no for an answer?

"I can manage, thank you. Besides, I'm sure you have lots of other things you could be doing on a Sunday morning."

Evan leaned against the edge of the folding table. "How do you know I'm not here to do my laundry?"

"Because you're not the kind of guy I figure would want to get arrested for indecent exposure — and the only clothes I see with you are the ones you're wearing."

Evan laughed. "Your kid sister told me you were here."

"I don't want to talk to you, Evan."

"Why not? What did I do?"

"Edie won't speak to me."

"She won't speak to me, either. So as long as we don't have anyone else to talk to, why don't we talk to each other?"

Brynn turned away from him and struggled to fold a sheet. Evan circled around her and grabbed one end.

"Let me help you," he said.

"No, thanks." She jerked the sheet away from him.

"Come on, Brynn. Don't be mad at me. I'm sorry about what happened last night. I know you're upset, but I don't think I did anything wrong."

She spread the sheet out on the table, and smoothed it down as best she could. Then she folded it. The result was lumpy and uneven.

"I can't help how I feel," he said. "I like you. I like you a lot. What's so terrible about that?"

She turned on him. "Don't you get it? Edie is my friend. My *best* friend."

"Then she shouldn't mind who you go out with."

"Up until two weeks ago she was your girlfriend."

"But she isn't any more."

"It doesn't matter. I can't go out with you, Evan. Not under these circumstances."

"What if the circumstances were different?"

She wished they were different. His eyes were so warm and she loved the way he looked when he smiled at her. But things were the way they were.

If she went out with him, Edie would be so hurt. And Edie was her best friend.

"Please go, Evan." She turned away from him, hoping that he'd get the message.

"Not until I tell you about Edie and me."

"It won't make any difference."

"Come on, Brynn, you're not like that. You don't make up your mind about something without even hearing the facts. You're a better person than that."

She whirled back around.

"All right," she said. She was angry at him for not understanding and for not leaving. "Go ahead and tell me about Edie and you. But I already know the whole story. And it won't make any difference."

His deep brown eyes hardened. He drew himself up stiff and straight. "I always thought you were a fair person. I thought you knew there were two sides to every story. But I guess I was wrong."

She'd never seen him angry. It startled her. "Evan . . . "

"Forget it," he said. He stalked out of the laundromat.

* * *

"Hi, Mrs. Spinelli. I gotta talk to Rita."

"Rita's still in bed, Chloe. Honestly, I don't know what that girl does that she needs so much sleep."

"I gotta see her right now, Mrs. Spinelli. It's important."

Mrs. Spinelli stepped aside to let her into the house. "While you're up there," she called as Chloe bounded up the stairs, "tell her I expect to see all her clothes hung up for a change or she won't get any allowance this month."

Yeah, sure, Mrs. Spinelli, thought Chloe. That's the most important thing I have to worry about today — where Rita puts her clothes. It was pretty funny, Chloe thought, considering that she couldn't remember where she had put her own.

She banged on Rita's door to give her fair warning in case she was sleeping in the nude. Rita always went on how she slept naked, and Chloe knew for a fact that there wasn't a boy in the whole school who hadn't repeated that story. It didn't make any difference to Chloe what Rita wore to bed, but she didn't particularly want to have to see her naked.

Rita was wearing pyjamas.

"Nice birthday suit," said Chloe as she sank down on the end of the bed.

"Busted," Rita said. "Don't tell, okay?" She yawned and stretched, rippling out her body like a cat's. "What time is it anyway?"

"Nearly one."

"So early?"

"Rita, you remember the sweater I had with me last night?"

Rita swore. "Chloe, you got me out of bed this early on a Sunday morning to talk about your clothes?"

"You're not out of bed," Chloe said, "and it's Sunday afternoon, not Sunday morning. And I need to know if you remember the sweater."

"Sure," said Rita. "It was red. And it had that little pin on it, the one with your initials."

Chloe felt as though the breath had been knocked out of her. She had forgotten about the pin.

"What's the matter, Chloe? You look funny all of a sudden."

"You remember where I left that sweater, Rita? You think maybe I left it on the mountain? I didn't leave it here, did I?"

"You weren't here last night, Chloe. We were at the pool hall, then we went to the mountain, remember?"

"And the restaurant," said Chloe. She felt sick inside. Rita frowned.

"We said we weren't ever going to mention that restaurant again. You promised."

"You remember where you last saw my sweater, Rita?"

"No! Chloe, what's the matter with you? Where are you going?"

"I have to find that sweater."

* * *

"Chloe! Hey, Chloe, are you here?"

Chloe heard Shadd's voice but she couldn't see him. Then he spoke again, more softly this time. His voice sounded like a low rumble. She couldn't make out the exact words. He must be talking to someone else. "Over here!" she called from behind the bushes where she was crouched, looking for her sweater. They were the same bushes she had sat behind with Shadd the night before, out of breath, trembling, wondering about the old man left lying behind the counter.

Shadd's head bobbed up above the greenery. Then Den's. It took another moment for Rita to appear, hobbling in a pair of new sandals.

"Geez, you guys," Rita said to Den, "it wouldn't have killed you to wait up a minute."

"You knew we were coming up here," said Den. "You should have worn sneakers." He turned to Chloe and fixed her with his green cat's eyes. "Hey, Chloe, what gives? What you doing way up here? It's not even dark."

"I'm looking for my sweater," said Chloe. Jerk. He already knew what she was doing, otherwise he wouldn't be up here.

"Did you find it?"

She shook her head. He came through the bushes and stood close to her. Too close. She stepped back to get away from him.

"Rita says you think you left it at the restaurant," he said.

Chloe scowled at Rita, who shrugged and stared down at the pink-painted toenails sticking out the ends of her new sandals. Geez, did she have to tell Den everything?

"All I know is, I had it with me last night," she said. "Now it's gone."

"Maybe you left it in the pool hall," Shadd said.

Chloe shook her head. "I already checked. It isn't there and the guy who was on duty last night, who

84

closed the place, he says he didn't see it."

"Then maybe it's around here somewhere. Or maybe somebody picked it up and took it home with them. It was a real nice sweater."

Now he decided to compliment her wardrobe. Some guys! "Yeah, sure, Shadd, maybe someone picked it up and took it home. Or maybe I left it at the restaurant and the police have it and they're looking for me right now."

"You didn't have your name sewn into it or any-thing, did you?" Den said.

"No. But I had a pin on it." She was sure Rita had already told him. But you never knew with Den. He liked to play these stupid little games, test you, see if he could catch you out. "It had my initials on it."

"Big deal. I bet lots of people have the initials *C.Y.* Must be a zillion of them in the city."

"Maybe," said Chloe. "But I bet there's not a zil-lion in the neighbourhood. If they start showing that sweater around, and that pin, maybe they'll find someone who recognizes it. Then what do you think is going to happen?"

"I know what I hope's *not* going to happen," Den said. He came close to her again, so close now that the end of her nose was practically touching his chest. "You're not going to rat on Shadd, are you, Chloe?"

"Nobody's going to rat on anybody," Shadd said. He slipped a hand around Chloe's shoulders. "Nobody has to say anything about anything. The old guy's going to be okay."

"The paper said he was unconscious. That sounds serious," Chloe said.

"Maybe that's what was in the morning paper," Shadd said. "I heard something different on the radio. They're saying he's going to be okay. So there's nothing to worry about."

"But the police were called in. What if they have my sweater?"

A smile flickered across Den's face. "If they have your sweater, then I guess that's your problem, Chloe."

"Thanks a hell of a lot."

Den made a hurt face. "Unless of course you want to turn the whole thing into Shadd's problem."

Chloe stared up into Shadd's eyes.

"Of course she doesn't," Shadd said. He peered down at Chloe, his arm still tight around her shoulders. "Come on, Chloe. Let's take a little walk." She let him steer her away from Den and Rita, over to a small clump of bushes. Shadd sat down and gestured for her to sit too. "Look, Chloe," he said, "the whole thing was a stupid accident. You know that, right?"

She nodded. "That's why I think we should go to the cops. To explain — "

Shadd cut her off with a shake of his head.

"No matter what we say now, it'll come out all twisted up. I heard the news. The old man says he was attacked by a gang of hoodlums. *Attacked*, Chloe. He was the one who started everything. He was coming at Den with that damn ladle again, ready to crack him another one on the head from behind. What was I supposed to do?"

"If we go to the cops and explain — "

"We can't. Don't you get it? The fact that we panicked last night and ran away just makes the old man's story sound true. If we go to the cops, my dad's going to have a stroke. He already told me, next time I get in trouble, any kind of trouble, he's going to make sure I get sent to one of those schools — you know, where they make you get up at six in the morning and do chores. They run those places practically like prisons, Chloe."

"But, Shadd — "

"I've already been kicked out of two schools, Chloe. Both times for fighting. I even got taken to court over one of them. The judge gave me a warning — "

"But you didn't do anything. Not on purpose. You were just trying to stop him from hitting Den."

"They got this thing called justifiable force, something like that. If a guy hits you and you hit him back, sometimes that's okay. It's like self-defence. But if a guy hits you with a feather and you deck him with a lead pipe, that's different. That's not self-defence. That's responding with an excess of force and you can get into trouble for that, especially if you got a file that looks like mine. And my old man? Geez, the cops bring me home one more time, and you can kiss me goodbye."

"But — "

"Besides, the old guy is going to be okay. All we

have to do is steer clear of his place and everything will be okay. How about it, Chloe?"

"I don't know, Shadd." Maybe what he said was true. Maybe the old man wasn't hurt that badly after all. But he was so old. And this morning the paper had said he was in serious condition. What if he suddenly keeled over and died? And what if the police got hold of her sweater with the pin on it and traced it back to her? She could just imagine her mother, hands on hips, saying, "I told you you'd get into trouble with that crowd, I told you so." For sure her mom wouldn't put up a fight on her behalf. Hell, she'd probably ask her new cop boyfriend if she could slap the handcuffs on Chloe herself.

"What about my sweater, Shadd?"

"You probably just misplaced it. Come on, I'll help you look for it."

He leaned forward and kissed her lightly on the cheek.

chapter 9

"Come on, Edie, you have to talk to me eventually," Brynn said. She slid around to the other side of Edie's locker. It was so childish. Edie kept turning her head away, forcing Brynn to dart from one side of the locker to make eye contact.

"We're in practically all of the same classes," Brynn said. "You're my lab partner in chemistry. You're going to have to talk to me eventually."

Edie turned slowly toward her. Her small grey eyes were cold and hard.

"I'm never going to speak to you again, Brynn," she said stiffly. "You and I are no longer friends."

"But I didn't do anything," Brynn said.

Edie clamped her mouth shut.

"Come on, Edie, if you won't talk to me, you can at least listen. It's not my fault that Evan keeps coming around. I didn't ask him to."

"Sure," said Edie snidely. "And I suppose it's not your fault that you were walking down the street with him the other night eating ice cream, either. I suppose you had nothing to do with that."

"He came over to my place," Brynn said, "and he started pestering me to go out with him — "

"And being the loyal friend you are, you immediately shoved aside any concern for me and my feelings and said yes. Gee, thanks a bunch, Brynn. If you ever need to be stabbed in the back, be sure to let me know. I'd be more than glad to return the favour."

"Edie, you're being unreasonable. I only agreed to go have some ice cream with him so that he'd leave me alone."

Edie's eyes narrowed. "Great plan," she said. "Too bad it didn't work."

"What do you mean?"

"I know you two were together in the laundromat yesterday. Don't even bother to deny it."

"Why would I deny it?" Brynn said. She was beginning to get angry. Edie didn't seem at all interested in hearing what had really happened. "I was at the laundromat doing the laundry and he just happened to walk in. It is a public place, you know."

Edie slammed her locker shut and inserted the lock through the door handle.

"Look," Brynn said, "it's obvious you're still in love with him — "

"I am not," Edie said. "I already told you, I don't care anything about that two-faced two-timer."

"Then why are you so mad?"

"Why am I mad?" Edie said. She stared at Brynn in disbelief. "Do I really have to explain it to you?"

"Edie — "

Edie adjusted her purse strap on her shoulder. "You and Evan O'Neill can go to hell for all I care," she said.

"Great," Brynn said. "That's just great." She gathered her own books closely to her chest and started off down the corridor just as the first bell of the morning rang.

* * *

Phoebe paused at the water fountain for a drink. She felt lightheaded when she bent over. When she straightened up again, everything suddenly went black and she had to grip the side of the fountain tightly to keep from falling over. Then the blackness was replaced by a million spots in a rainbow of colours dancing before her eyes. Phoebe's knuckles grew as white as the porcelain of the fountain bowl as she clung to it for balance.

"Hey," said a voice behind her, "are you all right?"

Phoebe nodded weakly. It took another few moments before her vision cleared enough so that she could see who was talking to her.

"Bobby." Her cheeks started to burn. "Oh, hi."

"Hi," Bobby said. He was frowning at her. "Are you sure you're okay? You look pale. Maybe you should go to the office, get a pass and go home."

"I'm okay," Phoebe said. But when she took her hand off the water fountain, her knees buckled. Bobby caught her by the elbow.

"I'll walk you to the office," he said. "If you don't want to go home, at least you should lie down for a while in the nurse's office."

"No, really," Phoebe protested, "I'm fine." Bobby's hand felt so warm on her arm.

"Are you sure?" he said.

She nodded.

"All right." He was still frowning. "Come on, then. I'll walk you to class."

Phoebe didn't argue. She felt wobbly and light-headed. Bobby kept a hand under her elbow, helping her along as if she were a frail old woman. Phoebe wished he were holding her hand instead, but this was almost as good. A couple of girls from Phoebe's class turned to stare as Bobby guided her carefully down the corridor toward homeroom.

"You should be careful," he said when they finally reached the door to the classroom. "You could be coming down with something. One time my older sister came down with the flu, but she didn't stay in bed the way any normal person would. She came to school and passed out at the top of a flight of stairs. She fell all the way down and broke her leg. My mom says she could just as easily have landed on her head, and then what?"

"That's terrible," Phoebe said.

Bobby shrugged. "My big sister can be a real pain. It was kind of neat to have her immobilized for a few weeks. But you, Phoebe . . . " Suddenly he was blushing furiously. Phoebe couldn't believe it. Then the homeroom bell clanged, startling both of them. Bobby almost jumped out of his skin. "I have to go," he said. "I'm going to be late."

* * *

Chloe spotted the back of Rita's head from halfway down the jammed corridor at lunchtime.

"Rita!" she called. "Hey, Rita, wait up!"

Rita turned, eyes scanning the mass of people in

the hallway before lighting on Chloe. She stopped and waited as the cafeteria-bound crowd swirled around her.

"Have you seen Shadd?" Chloe said when she finally reached her friend. "I went to pick him up at his locker, but he didn't show."

"Did he say he'd meet you there?"

"Well, no," Chloe said. "But he's usually hanging around there when I come by." For the past couple of weeks, she had been able to count on it. "Do you know if he came to school today?" That was the thing about dating a guy who was a grade ahead of her. She wasn't in any of his classes, so it was hard to keep track of where he was. "You don't think anything happened to him, do you?"

"I saw him just before the bell rang," Rita said. "Maybe he's already in the cafeteria."

"He usually waits for me."

Rita shrugged. "You know guys. Some days they're so hungry, they'd pass up an invitation to the Super Bowl just to get some food. Come on. I'm supposed to meet Den in the caf. Let's check it out. Maybe Shadd's there too."

The cafeteria was already packed. Everything at Earl Barron was always filled to capacity. The school had been built a few generations ago to accommodate approximately half the kids it held now. Year by year, class sizes had swollen. For a few years, school start times had been staggered, with the younger kids starting later than the older kids just so there would be enough classroom space for everyone. That had ended last year, but the place was still crowded. The cafeteria was the worst. There were two different lunch hours because it was impossible for all of the students to fit into the cafeteria at the same time. Even so, it was hard to find a seat unless you arrived as soon as the bell rang. Chloe had wasted a good ten minutes looking for Shadd.

"I hate this place," she said as she elbowed her way through the mob. "I feel like I'm in some over-populated Third World country every time I set foot in here."

"It could be worse," Rita said. "We could be starving."

"With the food they serve in here, I think I'd rather be starving." She pushed as far through the mob as she could, then strained to stand on tiptoe so that she could look up and down the rows for Shadd.

"You see him?" she asked.

"There's Den," Rita said. She started off toward him, but Chloe grabbed her by the elbow and yanked her back. "Is Shadd with him?"

Rita shook her head, then peered around. "If he's here, he must be hiding," she said, "because I don't — " Her voice broke off.

"You don't what?" Chloe said. "You're swallowing your words again, Rita."

"Nothing." When Rita turned back to face her, her face was almost scarlet.

"Are you okay?"

"I'm fine." She grabbed Chloe by the hand and started to drag her through the crowd. "Come on, let's go sit with Den. If Shadd's around, he'll find us."

"Ow," Chloe said. Rita's grip was too tight. "What's the matter with you?"

"I bet Den knows where he is. Come on, let's ask him."

Chloe jerked her arm free. The less she saw of Den, the better. "You go ask him," she said. "I'm going to look for Shadd."

"But Den can probably tell you — "

"I'll catch up with you later, Rita."

"But . . . "

She gave Rita a little push to send her on her way. Rita looked back through the crowd, with what Chloe thought was a miserable expression on her face. What was that about? Then Rita turned and began to work her way down the row of tables toward the back of the room where Den was sitting.

Chloe threaded a path through the crowd until she reached one side of the cafeteria. From there she had a relatively unobstructed view of the rows of tables and chairs. She began to scan them, starting on the far side of the room.

It took a few minutes but finally she spotted him. He was sitting at a table almost in the dead centre of the room, munching on a sandwich, a big grin on his face. It took Chloe another few moments to understand what he was smiling at. Or, rather, who. The girl opposite him was saying something, and Shadd was staring at her and smiling while she talked. As Chloe started to circle around toward him, she got a better look at the girl. She recognized her as a girl in Brynn's class — Penny something. Chloe didn't know her last name. A mane of thick golden hair hung down Penny's back. With one slim ivory hand, she reached across the table and touched Shadd's wrist. What was going on? Why was Shadd smiling at her like that? Chloe hurried down between the rows of chairs to where Shadd was sitting.

"Hi, Shadd," she said. "I've been looking all over for you."

Shadd almost dropped his chicken salad sandwich as he looked up at her.

"Chloe!" His cheeks reddened. "Hey, hi." He glanced at the girl, Penny, and shrugged as if he didn't know why Chloe was there or what she wanted. What was going on? "So, how are things?" he said.

"I don't know," Chloe said. She looked at the other girl. "You tell me. I've been looking all over for you. I thought you were going to meet me at your — " One glance at Shadd and the way he was looking at Penny silenced her.

"You're Brynn's sister, aren't you?" Penny said. She smiled at Chloe, but it was all for show. There was no real feeling behind it. "I don't mean to be rude or anything," she said. "But Shadd and I are having a private conversation."

Chloe looked back in confusion at Shadd. "What

is going on?" she demanded.

"He's busy right now, that's what's going on," Penny said.

"Chloe — " Shadd began. But it was too late. She had already turned and was making her way back through the jungle of chairs and tables and people.

chapter 10

Once she had fought her way out of the cafeteria, Chloe started to run. She didn't care that it was strictly against school regulations. She didn't care that Mr. Chisholm and Mr. Rusnek, the school vice-principals, regularly patrolled the hallways at lunchtime, handing out detentions for infractions of those regulations. All she wanted was to get away, fast.

She heard footsteps behind her and glanced back over her shoulder. It was Shadd. Well, tough, she thought. He'd had his chance. She didn't want to talk to him. She threw herself against the exit door and exploded out into the asphalt of the school-yard.

The schoolyard was almost as packed as the cafeteria. Now that the weather was nice, lots of kids took their lunches outside. Chloe darted through the clumps of people and headed for the break in the chain link fence that circled the yard. Then a hand grabbed her and jerked her back. "Come on, Chloe," Shadd said. "I want to talk to you."

"Let me go," Chloe said.

"Not until you tell me why you took off like that."

"Right. Like you can't figure it out yourself. We always meet at your locker, Shadd. I looked for you everywhere. I waited. You didn't show up, I got worried. I thought maybe the cops — " She broke off and looked up at him. "And when I finally go look-ing for you, where do I find you? Down in the cafe-teria with that snot-face Penny what's-her-name." She yanked herself free of his grip, but he caught her again and held fast.

"I thought we were supposed to meet in the cafe-teria. I thought that's what you said." He sounded so desperate for her to believe him that it almost knocked her off balance. "Honest, Chloe. Hey, when was the last time I ever stood you up?" He peered into her eyes and gently let his hand fall away from her arm. "Come on, Chloe, you know how I feel about you."

"So what were you doing with Penny?"

"Nothing. I was waiting for you."

"She said you were having a *private* conversa-tion. What was that all about?"

Shadd reached out with both hands as he shook his head, catching Chloe's hands in his. "Nothing important," he said. He pulled her gently toward him.

"What were you even doing sitting with her?"

"Did it ever occur to you that I was sitting there waiting for you and she just slid into the seat I was saving for you and started talking to me? Did that ever occur to you?" His biceps rippled as he pulled her a little closer. He was so strong, it was hard to hold back.

"Why would she just sit down and start talking to you?" Chloe asked as she was drawn slowly closer and closer.

Shadd smiled. He leaned down and kissed her gently on the lips. "I don't know," he murmured. "Maybe she wanted to find out if I had any plans for the dance."

Before Chloe could ask him whether he did, he kissed her again, harder this time, and wrapped his arms around her.

* * *

Phoebe's head started pounding halfway through French, her last class of the day. When the final bell rang at last, she got up from her seat and hurried for the door. The only thing she could think of was getting home as fast as possible and making a nice cup of tea to drink with her SlimNow. Maybe she'd take a couple of aspirins too, for her headache. Maybe then she'd start feeling better.

She made her way shakily down the crowded hallway. It was the end of the school day, so everyone was in a good mood, chattering, laughing. But the voices seemed to ring more loudly than usual in her ears, and the faces and bodies swam around her. As she came to the head of the stairs, Phoebe groped for support from the banister. Her knees began to buckle. Everything went black.

* * *

The whole thing was so stupid that Brynn hadn't been able to stop thinking about it all day. Edie was mad at her because the boyfriend she claimed to care nothing about was making advances that Brynn was doing her level best to discourage. She didn't even bother going back to Edie's locker after school. If Edie had anything to say to her, she could come looking for her. There was no way Brynn was going to keep apologizing for something that wasn't her fault. She'd proved she wasn't interested in Evan, hadn't she? She kept refusing to see him, didn't she? What more did Edie want? She tightened her grip on her school books as she headed for the stairs up to the second floor where her locker was.

She wasn't even sure what it was that caught her eye. Maybe the flash of blue. Maybe the startled yelp of a girl halfway up the stairs. Whatever it was, she turned and saw Phoebe toppling down the concrete stairs, her arms and legs hitting each step like the lifeless limbs of a rag doll. Brynn dropped her books and ran for the stairs.

* * *

It was that cop again. Although her mother had said she was expecting him, Chloe was still surprised to see him. Most of Sheila's boyfriends didn't last very long.

"She's not home yet," Chloe shouted through the closed door. Levesque just smiled blandly as if he hadn't heard, and stared at her expectantly, waiting for her to open the door. What was wrong with some people, Chloe wondered as she unlocked the door. Did they have to have everything explained to them? Couldn't they figure anything out for themselves? Geez, and he was a cop. A detective. You'd think he could deduce something. "I said she's not home yet."

"That's okay," he said as he stepped into the front hall. "She's expecting me. I don't mind waiting."

Chloe blocked his way. She didn't want to have to entertain a cop for heaven knew how long. "The thing is, I don't know when she's going to be home. She went to the hospital," she said.

His face clouded. "Did something happen?"

"My sister had an accident."

"Which sister? Brynn?"

"Phoebe. She fell down some stairs — "

"Is she all right?" He sounded almost as if he cared.

"I don't know. She fainted or something and fell, and Mom tore out of here to go to the hospital." In fact, Chloe had been astonished by how quickly her mother had moved after she hung up the phone. She'd dashed out of the apartment without even freshening her lipstick or running a brush through her hair, and had called up to Chloe only as an afterthought to let Levesque in if he arrived before she returned.

"What hospital is she in?" Levesque said. "I'll go over, see if she needs anything."

"No, she said you should — " Chloe began before she realized what she was saying. Levesque gave her that look again, patient and waiting. "She said you should wait here and if it didn't look like she'd be back soon, she'd call."

"I see," Levesque said. "Then I suppose I'd better wait." Finally Chloe had to stand aside. Annoyed, she waved him into the living room.

"Can I get you anything?" Mostly she wanted an excuse to get away from him.

"No, thank you."

"Well then," she said, sliding toward the door. "You don't mind if I leave you alone in here, do you? Finals are coming up. I have to study."

"No problem," he said. "Studies are important for young people."

Chloe nodded. She wondered what he had been like when he was young, whether he'd had his nose stuck in a book the whole time, or whether he'd gone out for football. He was a big guy, but she couldn't imagine a football player saying something as school-teacherish as what he had just said. She started to turn away from him.

"Tell me, Chloe," he said. "Are there many Asian girls in your school?"

What kind of question was that? She turned back slowly. "There are a few. Why?"

He wore a placid smile, but his eyes were sharp and probing. "An old man was assaulted around here on Saturday night. Have you heard anything about that?"

"No," Chloe said. "What old man? And what does that have to do with Asian girls?"

"An old man who owns a restaurant a few blocks from here. He was badly hurt. He says some kids came into his place and started some rough stuff. Apparently they pushed him down. He almost fractured his skull when he fell against the edge of his grill stove." He was drilling into her with his eyes.

Chloe regarded him impassively, waiting for him to continue. "The old man says that one of the members of the gang that attacked him was an Asian girl."

"Oh," Chloe said. "Well, I bet if went to the principal at my school, he'd give you a list of all the Asian girls with their addresses and phone numbers. Or are you asking me because you think that since we all look the same, we all hang around together?"

She was trying to embarrass him, but it didn't work.

"I'm asking you because I thought you might have heard something," he said. "I thought you might know the girl."

"Well, I don't." She turned again to leave.

"Where were you Saturday night?" Levesque said.

Chloe swallowed hard and took a deep breath before turning to face him again. "I was out."

"Alone?"

"With some friends." She tried to stay calm. "And we weren't anywhere near any restaurant, in case that's what you're thinking. We spent the whole night up on the mountain." She hoped that would put an end to his questions, but it didn't.

"How many friends were you with?"

He looked straight at her, and she knew that she had to look straight back at him so that he wouldn't think she was trying to hide anything. She should have said she was alone. That way, he couldn't try to trip her up. But it was too late for that now. She shrugged and tried to sound like it was no big deal when she said, "A couple. Why?"

"If I asked you for the names of your friends, you'd give them to me?"

Chloe shrugged with what she hoped looked like indifference, and said, "Sure." She hoped he wouldn't ask. "But what for? You think I was involved?"

He looked at her evenly for a few moments. Then he said, "What are their names?"

Geez, she definitely should have told him she was alone, because now if she refused to tell him who she was with, he'd get suspicious. But if she gave him any names, he would check them out, or get some other cops to check them out.

"Don't you remember who you were with on Saturday night?"

"Sure," she said. "I was with my friend Rita and her boyfriend."

"What's her boyfriend's name?"

Geez. "Den."

"Den what?"

"Whitman. Dennis Whitman."

"And what's Rita's last name?"

"Spinelli."

"They live around here?"

She nodded.

"They go to your school?"

She nodded again.

"And that's it, there were just you and Rita and Den?"

"Yeah." She didn't want to give Shadd's name, not after what he had said his father would do if he got into any more trouble. Besides, the old guy had probably told the police it was two boys and two girls, and if she insisted there were just the three of them, maybe she'd be okay. For sure Den wouldn't give anything away. He'd say he was on the mountain. She wasn't so sure about Rita, though.

"Mind if I use your telephone?"

"Go ahead," Chloe said. "It's in the kitchen."

She continued out of the room as he got up and went into the kitchen, but she stopped just outside the entrance to the living room, straining her ears and holding her breath. It didn't do any good. She couldn't hear what he was saying. But she was pretty sure who he was talking to.

* * *

The curtain swooshed shut and Phoebe heard the *click click* of her mother's heels on the tile as she went off in search of a telephone. As Phoebe struggled to get out of the open-backed hospital gown and into her clothes, Brynn watched her. It made Phoebe feel embarrassed. She wasn't used to dressing in front of an audience.

"You look awfully pale to me," Brynn said. "Are you sure you're feeling okay?"

"I'm fine," Phoebe said. "Could you turn around?"

"What for?"

Phoebe rolled her eyes.

"Oh," Brynn said. She shrugged. "Sure. I hope

you're going to watch where you're going from now on. You scared everyone to death. When I called Mom to tell her you'd been taken to the hospital, she started to cry."

"It's not my fault," Phoebe said. "I tripped."

"Are you sure that's what happened?"

The question startled Phoebe. Brynn was looking at her so intently it was scary.

"Jenny Churchill was right behind you and she said it looked to her like you fainted. She said you just kind of crumpled at the top of the stairs."

"Jenny Churchill wears glasses this thick," Phoebe said, holding her thumb and forefinger a good distance apart. "And she still has to hold a book pressed right up to her nose before she can see anything."

"So you didn't faint?"

"I tripped."

Brynn studied her again. "You look pale. Are you sure you're okay? Maybe you're coming down with something."

"Brynn, this is a hospital. I just saw a doctor. Don't you think if there was something wrong, he would have found it? I told you, I tripped."

"Okay," Brynn said. But she didn't look satisfied.

"Knock, knock," a cheery voice on the other side of the curtain called. A nurse poked her head through. "You have a visitor, Phoebe."

Phoebe frowned. Who could possibly come to visit her in an emergency room?

Bobby Keough stumbled through the curtains, a

small bouquet of pink carnations in his hand.

"Hi, Phoebe," he said. He thrust the flowers awkwardly at her. "I brought you something to cheer you up."

Phoebe beamed at him. "That's so sweet. Thank you, Bobby."

"Guess this is my cue to take off," Brynn said.

* * *

Brynn stepped into the busy hospital corridor to wait, and there he was, just like that. In the sea of strange faces that surrounded her, she found one she knew, and was happy to see it. "What are you doing here, Evan?" she asked.

"Somebody told me you came to the hospital in an ambulance."

She was touched by the concern she saw in his eyes. "Phoebe came in an ambulance," she said. "I just rode along with her, to make sure she was going to be okay."

Relief chased away worry. "So you're not hurt or sick or anything?"

"I'm fine."

He broke into a smile. "Great," he said. "That's wonderful. Because I thought — " He looked down at the floor and shuffled awkwardly. She wanted to ask him what he had thought, but she was afraid of what he might say.

"It was nice of you to come, Evan," she said.

"You're not mad at me?"

"For showing up at the hospital to check on me?"

"For showing up, period."

"I'm not mad," she said.

"Why won't you go out with me?"

Not that again. "I already told you, Evan. You were going out with Edie. What you did — you broke her heart."

Evan slapped the wall in frustration. "Edie again. Every time I try to talk to you, you tell me about Edie. So what happens now? For the rest of my life no one will ever go out with me because I went out with Edie a few times?"

"I'm sure someone will go out with you, Evan. Just not me."

"Geez, come on, Brynn."

"She's my best friend."

"If she really was your best friend, she wouldn't be telling you who you could see and who you couldn't. She's unhappy, so she's trying to make sure no one else is happy. She's being manipulative, Brynn. She's good at that."

"If you feel that way about her," Brynn said, "why did you start going out with her in the first place?"

"I didn't." The exasperation was growing in his voice. "I mean, I went out with her, sure. But I didn't really think of it as going out, you know, like she was my girlfriend or anything, until she made a big deal about it. You know?"

"No," Brynn said. "I don't know. Are you saying that all the time you were going out with Edie, you didn't even want to be with her?"

"Sort of," Evan said. He looked at her. "Yeah. It sounds pretty terrible, doesn't it? I just — I don't know — I guess I didn't want to hurt her feelings."

She stared at him a moment. "You went out with her because you didn't want to hurt her feelings?"

"It's more like I didn't *stop* going out with her because I didn't want to hurt her feelings. Whenever I tried to break it off, she'd start to cry ... Boy, I must sound so lame."

"It doesn't make any difference, Evan. It would just kill her — and our friendship — if I went out with you."

Evan's whole body sagged. "You really mean it, don't you?" he said. "You're never going to go out with me."

"I'm sorry, Evan. Maybe we can still be friends ... "

"But not good enough friends to go to the dance together, right? Because Edie's not going, you can't go?"

"Evan — "

"Because Edie says no, you won't go. All Edie has to do is snap her fingers — "

"Evan!"

"I'm sorry," he said. "I'm sorry. But that's what it feels like."

"I'm sorry, too," Brynn said.

"Yeah. I can tell. You're all broken up over it." He started to turn away, then paused to look at her. "It's too bad. I bet we would have made a great couple. And you know what the funny thing is? I wanted to tell you that four months ago, at Danny Brossard's party. But I never got the chance. Edie told me she was afraid to walk home alone so Mrs.

Brossard asked me to walk her. And the next thing I knew, it's all over school that I'm going out with her." He walked away.

chapter 11

Chloe was sure she would go crazy waiting for Levesque to leave. For the first time in a long time, she was happy to pick up the phone and hear her mother's voice. Because she could predict what would happen next.

"She wants to talk to you," Chloe said as she handed Levesque the receiver.

She was surprised by the concern in his eyes as he asked her mother gentle questions. He really seemed to care about Phoebe's condition and how Sheila was bearing up. That made him a lot different from most of the men her mother went out with. They didn't usually care about anything except getting out of the apartment with her as fast as possible.

"I'm going to the hospital to get your mother and sisters," he said as he hung up the phone. "Do you want to come?"

"No, thanks."

She was dialling Rita's number before Levesque's footsteps had faded on the stairs.

"She's not here," Rita's mother said.

"Do you know where she is?"

It was a stupid question. Rita's mother never seemed to know where Rita was, unless she happened to be sitting right next to her.

"I think she and Dennis went out somewhere,"

was the best Rita's mother had to offer.

Somewhere? They could be anywhere. Chloe grabbed her keys and took off down to Mount Royal. If she was lucky, she'd find them in a pool hall. Or maybe sitting out in the park eating ice cream.

She wasn't lucky. By nine o'clock she still hadn't found them. But at least she had narrowed the field. Rita's curfew was nine-thirty on a school night, and Den almost always walked her home. Chloe decided to go over to Rita's house to wait.

A police cruiser sat at the curb outside the squat stone house where Rita lived. Chloe ducked back behind a bus stand when she saw it. Oh, no. Maybe they'd talked to Rita already. Or maybe they were waiting to talk to *her*. Maybe she was too late.

She peeked out from her hiding place and saw two uniformed officers coming down a flight of stairs. But it wasn't Rita's stairs they were coming down. It was a house two doors down. They walked directly to their car, got in and drove away. Chloe let out a sigh of relief.

"Braughhh!"

A hand clamped itself over Chloe's eyes, another over her mouth. Chloe froze in terror. Then she heard Rita's soft giggle.

"Very funny," she mumbled under Den's hand.

"It is from where I stand," Den said.

"What are you doing here?" Rita asked.

"I've been looking for you guys."

"Yeah, well, you found us. What's up?" said Den.

Chloe hesitated. Den wasn't going to like this. "The cops might be wanting to ask you some questions."

Den frowned. "What about?"

"About the other night. About the old man."

"Yeah?" Den stared suspiciously at Chloe. "And why would they want to question us? Nobody saw us there."

"The old man told them one of the kids was Asian. In case you haven't noticed, Den, there aren't that many Asians in the neighbourhood."

"You mean they came looking for you?" Rita asked.

Chloe nodded. "Sort of."

"What do you mean, sort of? Did you go to the cops, Chloe?"

"Of course not. How stupid do you think I am?"

"What then?"

"I told you. This cop started asking me some questions — "

"What cop?"

"What difference does it make, what cop? It was just a cop."

"The cop your mom's going with?" Rita said. Chloe could have strangled her. She should never have told Rita about Levesque.

Den's eyes narrowed. "Your mother's going out with a *cop?*" He stepped in closer to Chloe. "What did you tell him?"

"He asked me if I knew any Asian girls. Then he asked me where I was Saturday night."

"And?"

"And I told him I was with you."

Den made a sour face. "Brilliant," he said. "Just brilliant."

"I told him I was with you and Rita, period," Chloe said. "So if they ask you, don't mention Shadd. That way they'll get the idea that it was only the three of us and that we weren't anywhere near the place."

"What difference does it make?" said Rita. She had a panicky look in her eyes. "They think we did it, don't they?"

"They think four kids did it. Three white kids and an Asian. If we stick to the story that the three of us were together on the mountain, we'll be okay."

"You sure about that?" Den said.

"Sure I'm sure," Chloe said. But she wasn't. What if Levesque or some other cop decided to show her picture to the old man? Would he recognize her?

"Oh my God," Rita said. "The cops are going to know we did it. We're going to get arrested, aren't we? My mother's going to kill me."

"The cops are not going to arrest us," Den said impatiently. "We didn't do anything. That old guy's all right. He didn't die or anything."

"The cops think Shadd assaulted the guy," Chloe said.

"They already know it was Shadd?" Rita's face went pale. "Oh my God. What if he tells them — "

"That's not what I mean," Chloe said. She wished Rita would calm down.

"But you said — "

"I meant that the cops think *someone* assaulted the guy. They don't know who. But if they find out Shadd did it, they'll charge him. They could even charge us for obstructing a police investigation or something, you know, if we lie to them and they find out about it."

"Great," Den said. "Whose side are you on?"

"What do you mean?" Rita said. She looked frantically from Den to Chloe. "You're not going to tell the cops, are you, Chloe?"

Chloe rolled her eyes.

Den smiled. "She's not going to tell the cops," he said. "She already lied to them. And that's exactly what we're going to do, baby." He slipped an arm around Rita's waist. "Shadd's old man'll come down hard if Shadd's in any more trouble. We don't want that to happen. Do we, Chloe?"

* * *

One nice thing about falling headfirst down that flight of stairs, thought Phoebe, was that her mother was letting her stay home today. What wasn't so nice, though, was that her mother couldn't stay with her.

"I promised I'd cover a few shifts for Yvette," she said. "But I'll call you, honey, okay?"

Phoebe remembered the time when she'd had the chicken pox. Her mother had stayed home with her then and had read to her and fed her clear broth. She wished she were six years old again. But, she thought as she listened to her mother's footsteps fading down the front steps, *at least I have the whole place to myself.* She couldn't remember the last time that had happened. There was TV if she wanted to watch TV. There was music to listen to. And she didn't have to think about school at all, because somehow in all the excitement her school books hadn't made their way home. She had nothing to study even if she felt like studying, which she didn't.

Every bone in her body seemed to ache. She had an angry purple and blue bruise on one hip, and another patch of black on one knee. Her head throbbed. And her stomach growled.

She stayed in bed for an hour, feeling the ache in her belly, but not ready to risk the ache in her bones if she tried to get up. Finally the hunger became unbearable. She struggled into a sitting position and let out a yelp when the swollen skin stretched over her bruised hip. She had never hurt herself so badly before. She hoped she never would again.

She walked slowly, one hand on the wall to steady herself as she made her way down the hall to the kitchen. She fumbled with the kettle in the sink, managed to fill it, and set it onto the stove to boil. A nice cup of tea and a couple of SlimNows, and she'd be just fine. While she waited for the kettle, she reached up to open the cupboard where the tea was kept.

Her mother must have done some shopping yesterday, thought Phoebe, because right there at the front of the shelf was a package of chocolate chip cookies. Phoebe pulled it out of the way so that she could get at the tea. After she found the tea canister and brought it down to the counter, she picked up the bag of cookies, meaning to replace it on the shelf. She hesitated. She loved chocolate chip cookies. And this brand was her favourite. The cookies had more chips than any other kind you could buy, and lots of walnuts too.

One cookie wouldn't hurt. She had eaten practically nothing for days. She was losing weight. She knew because her pants weren't tight around her waist anymore. One cookie would be a sort of reward for how hard she had been working.

She opened the bag and took one. She held it to her nose and smelled it. There was nothing like the fragrance of chocolate. Her mouth began to water.

She nibbled off the tiniest taste, and intended to eat the whole cookie that way. Savour it. Make it last. But as the chocolate melted against her tongue, she took another bite, a bigger one. And then another. Then suddenly the cookie was gone. She had eaten it all.

She opened the cupboard door again and stared at the package. How many calories were there in just one cookie? She strained to remember what she had read in her calorie-counter book. One chocolate chip cookie, a hundred and fifty calories, something like that. So one more wouldn't hurt. Three hundred calories wasn't much. If she didn't eat anything else, she would still lose weight.

She pulled the bag down again and ate another cookie.

* * *

"Sit down, Edie," Brynn said.

Edie scrunched her lunch bag in one hand, but did not sit.

"You planning on doing this for the rest of your life?" Brynn went on. "You going to run away every time I come around?"

"I told you, you're not my friend any more." Edie turned to walk away.

"I saw Evan last night."

Edie spun around to face her. "You *what?*"

"I saw Evan last night. And I told him not to bother me any more. Edie, I don't want to go out with Evan. Really. But I *do* want to be your friend. Please?"

Edie eyed her speculatively a moment. "Really?" she said at last. "You told him that?"

"I told him."

"What did he say?"

"He said he understood," Brynn said. She didn't like telling lies, but this one was definitely at the white end of the spectrum. She was only telling it to protect Edie's feelings. "So that's the end of that. Everything's taken care of. Now can't we please be friends?"

Edie bit her lower lip. She pulled out the empty chair opposite Brynn. She smiled as she dropped onto it. "I'm sorry," she said. "I know you probably think I've been acting like such a jerk . . . "

Brynn shrugged. "You know what else?" she said.

"What?"

"Mickey Shea's staring at you."

A blush crept up Edie's neck. "You're kidding," she said. "Where is he?"

Brynn nodded toward the aisle to her right. "He's been staring at you ever since you sat down. I think maybe he's got a thing for you."

Edie's cheeks were scarlet, but she beamed with pleasure. "You think so? You think maybe he's interested in me?"

Brynn smiled. It was good to see Edie happy again, and it was good to be able to talk to her again.

"Sure," she said. "Maybe he heard you were available. Maybe that's why he's staring."

* * *

Phoebe peered into the bag again and still couldn't believe it. It was empty. Completely empty. She had eaten all the cookies. Three dozen of them. And it hadn't even taken her that long.

She couldn't believe she had done something so terrible — and after she had been so good for so long. After she had cut her calories down to practically zero. In less than an hour she had managed to consume all the calories that she had so labouriously cut out of her diet for the past three days. It wasn't fair. It couldn't be happening, not after she had been trying so hard.

Maybe she could undo what she had done. Maybe she could reverse the damage. She ran to the toilet, threw herself down and rammed her fingers down her throat. She gagged, and then she vomited.

* * *

"Rita? Did you hear what I said? You're wanted in the office, Rita." Mr. Howison looked down the aisle at her. He had been interrupted in mid-equation by a knock at the door. One of the school secretaries had handed him a note. "Get a move, Rita. Don't keep everyone waiting."

Rita cast a frantic glance at Chloe as she got up from her seat. She walked slowly up the aisle and out of the room. By the end of math class, she still hadn't returned. Chloe bundled up Rita's books along with her own, and carried them down to the first floor for history.

Halfway through Mrs. Galloway's class, Rita slipped through the door, handed a note to Mrs. Galloway, and slunk to her desk. She didn't look up for the rest of class, and she refused to look at Chloe, no matter how many bits of eraser Chloe lobbed at her.

When the bell rang, Rita grabbed her books and made a break for the door. Chloe chased after her, caught her by the arm and hauled her over to the nearest exit door.

"Hey," yelped Rita as Chloe shoved her out into the asphalt schoolyard. "You're going to get us suspended."

"What did they want at the office?"

Rita shifted her gaze to the ground. "It was the cops," she said. "They wanted to ask me some questions."

"And?" said Chloe.

Rita glanced angrily at her. "And I answered them," she said. "What do you think?"

"What did you tell them?"

"I told them what you said. That you and me and Den were up on the mountain all night." Her gaze wavered a moment, then gave way.

"What else did you tell them?" Chloe asked.

"Nothing. I just told them what I said."

"But?"

Rita looked at her in anguish. "But I don't think they believed me. I'm a terrible liar, Chloe. I've always been a terrible liar."

Chloe stared evenly at Rita. "Have they talked to Den yet?" she asked.

"I don't know."

"Okay, well, don't panic. Den's a good liar. He's almost as good as me."

chapter 12

Chloe couldn't find Shadd. When she went to his locker, someone told her that he had just left. The same thing happened when she tried to catch him right after class.

"Shadd?" they said. "You just missed him."

She knew it probably had something to do with what she'd said to the cops. For sure Den would have told him by now. But she hadn't said anything that would get him into trouble. She wanted to make sure he understood that, and she didn't trust Den to deliver the message.

When the last bell rang for the day, she flew down the hallway, not even caring if Rusnek gave her a detention for running. As she rounded the corner down near the stairs, she crashed right into Philomen. He bounced backward, staggered and fell onto the floor.

"Oh, no. Sorry, Phil," she said.

He blinked up at her, then struggled to his feet.

"Are you okay?"

"I'm fine," he said. But he looked dazed. She bent to help him retrieve the books that had scattered on impact. She looked at him again. For the first time that she could remember, he wasn't smiling.

"You don't sound fine," she said. "Are you hurt?"

He shook his head.

"My grandfather was beaten up," he said.

"What?"

"My grandfather. He owns a small restaurant. Maybe you know it. It's very close to here."

Chloe felt a chill seeping through her. "No," she said. "I don't even like Chinese food."

Philomen was staring at her intently. She couldn't even begin to guess what he was thinking. It made her feel uncomfortable.

"A gang of hooligans beat up my grandfather. He was in the hospital for several days. He won't be able to go back to his restaurant for two weeks because he is old and he needs to rest."

"That's terrible, Phil," Chloe said. "Really terrible. Does your grandfather have any idea who they were?"

Philomen shook his head. "But my grandfather says there were four of them and he says one was Chinese."

Chloe forced a smile. "There's not many Chinese people around here. I guess they won't have much trouble finding whoever did it, huh?"

"There was a sweater in the restaurant," Philomen said. "The police said it might help them find who did this to my grandfather." He didn't sound very hopeful.

"A sweater, eh?" It was a struggle to keep the smile on her lips and the casual lilt in her voice. "How's a sweater going to help them? Did it have a name in it or something?"

Philomen stared at her for a moment and then shook his head. "But the police told me that sometimes things like that can help them."

"Without a name in it?" Chloe said. "Not even any initials?"

Philomen shook his head again.

* * *

"You know what we could do?" Edie said. "We could go out for supper. To a really nice place. Then we could go to a movie. Then maybe we could take a buggy ride on the mountain. And then — "

Brynn laughed. "Where do you suggest we get the money to do all of that?" she asked. "Or are we going to start the day off by robbing a bank?"

"We could use the money I saved up for a dress. And I was going to get my hair done."

"Oh, no, Edie. You don't have to — "

Edie forced a brave smile. "It's okay," she said. "It's no big deal. Hey, who knows, maybe if we go to a nice restaurant, we'll meet some guys. Maybe we won't end up taking that buggy ride alone."

Brynn laughed. "You're hopeless," she said.

"A hopeless romantic," Edie said, and sighed.

Brynn pushed the door open and they stepped out into the late afternoon sunshine. This time of year she loved going outside. The air was getting warmer every day, the air was scented with leaves and grass, and birds chirped in every tree.

"You want to go down to the park?" she said.

Edie jabbed her in the ribs with an elbow.

"Hey, you could just say no . . . "

"That vermin," Edie said between clenched teeth. "That miserable rotten — Over there." She pointed.

Brynn looked across the schoolyard and caught her breath when she saw where Edie was pointing.

"He doesn't waste any time, does he? As soon as one girl loses interest in him, he's off chasing another one."

Evan was sitting on the asphalt in the shade of an old maple. Next to him was Angeline Phillips, her skirt stopped short at mid-thigh, her legs slim and already tan.

"Ten to one he's asking her to the dance," Edie said.

Brynn stared at him. It couldn't be true. He couldn't really be interested in Angeline, not so soon. But he was smiling as he talked to her, and Angeline was gazing intently into his eyes.

Suddenly, he looked up. His eyes met Brynn's. She waited for him to jump to his feet, to distance himself from Angeline, to at least try to give Brynn the impression that he wasn't interested in Angeline. But he didn't. Instead, he smiled at Brynn, stretched out an arm and dropped it onto Angeline's shoulder. Angeline's smile widened.

"He's disgusting," Edie said.

Brynn felt a knot form in the pit of her stomach.

"Come on," Edie said. "Let's get out of here."

* * *

"I told your mother I'd drop in on you," the big policeman said. Phoebe stared up at him. He was so big and his voice was so deep that she was a little afraid of him, although she knew her mother liked him a lot. "She's worried about you."

126

Phoebe blinked in surprise. It wasn't like her mother's boyfriends to care about her kids.

"You look pale. Are you hungry?" he asked. "Would you like me to make you something to eat?"

Phoebe shook her head miserably. The last thing she wanted to do was eat.

"Come on," Levesque said. "Come into the kitchen with me and we'll see what we can find."

She trailed along helplessly behind him. He was so big and he was a policeman. He probably wasn't used to people saying no to him. Phoebe bit her lip and watched as he opened one cupboard after another until he found a tin of soup.

"This will be good for you," he said. He rummaged in a drawer and pulled out a can opener. "You just sit down there, Phoebe. I'll have some soup ready for you in no time."

"I'm really not very hungry," she said in a small voice.

"Nonsense," Levesque said. "We'll get a little soup into you and before you know it, you'll feel like your old self again."

He pulled a pot from the drawer under the stove, poured the container of soup into it and set it down onto the heat. "Your mother seems worried about you," he said again as he stirred the pot. He turned to study her a moment. "How are you feeling today?"

"I'm fine," Phoebe said. But he didn't look convinced.

"You look sick," he said. "Are you sure your sister

wasn't right?" When she looked at him in confusion, he explained. "Brynn said that one of your friends told her it looked like you fainted. Are you sure you didn't faint?"

"I tripped," Phoebe said. But she couldn't look him in the eye when she said it.

Levesque turned away from her to stir the soup.

"Sometimes," he said, "when something like that happens, you don't remember afterward. Maybe you fainted. Maybe that's why you look so pale now. Ah, soup's ready."

He found a bowl and a spoon, set them onto the table, then ladled out a helping of thick, rich soup. Phoebe stared down at the chunks of carrot and potato and at the fat, slippery noodles. The last thing she wanted was to put anything else into her stomach.

"I promised your mother that I wouldn't leave until you had had at least one bowlful," Levesque said. He sat down on the chair opposite hers. "Eat up now."

She lifted the spoon and took a tiny sip of the soup. It seared her throat as she swallowed it.

"Did I tell you that I once had a little girl?" Levesque said.

Phoebe shook her head. She knew nothing at all about him. "Are you married?" she asked.

He shook his head. "But I was once. And I had a little girl. You remind me a lot of her."

The spoon hung in Phoebe's hand. Her stomach churned from just the small mouthful she had swallowed. "Why?" she asked miserably. "Was she fat?"

The question seemed to take Levesque by surprise. "She had pretty eyes just like yours," he said. "And pretty hair. Would you like to see a picture of her?"

Phoebe nodded. She was willing to do anything if it meant that she wouldn't have to eat any more soup.

Levesque dug into his pocket and brought out a wallet. He opened it and pulled out a small photograph, which he handed to Phoebe.

Phoebe studied the girl whose face looked out at her. She did indeed have blond hair and blue eyes like Phoebe. She was wearing a bathing suit and squinting into the sunlight; on her face she wore a big smile. If anything, she was even chunkier than Phoebe.

"Where is she now?" Phoebe asked as she returned the picture.

"She died. She was very sick and she died."

"What about your wife? Where is she?"

"She's married to someone else."

He stared for a moment at the photograph before slipping it back into his wallet. Phoebe wondered how long ago the girl had died, but she didn't dare to ask.

"I think you should eat your soup," Levesque said. "And then I think you should take very good care of yourself. Your mother would be very unhappy if anything bad happened to you."

chapter 13

"Yuck!" Chloe exclaimed as she came into the kitchen. "What's been going on in the bathroom? Has somebody been puking in there?"

Phoebe's cheeks started to redden. Brynn glanced over at her from the sink where she was peeling potatoes. "Phoebe? Are you sick?"

"No," Phoebe said quickly. But Brynn didn't seem satisfied. She dried her hands on a towel and pressed one cool palm to Phoebe's forehead.

"Hey, did anyone call me?" Chloe asked, oblivious to the exchange between her sisters.

"No," Brynn said. Her eyes were on Phoebe. "Are you sure you're not sick?" she asked.

"Yes," Phoebe said. "I told you. I feel like I've been telling everyone in the whole world. I'm fine."

"Look, you sure Shadd didn't call?" Chloe reached up to open the cupboard above the sink.

"I'm sure," Brynn said. "And stay out of the cupboard. We're going to have supper as soon as Mom gets home."

But Chloe didn't close the cupboard. She rooted around on the shelf. "Hey, where are the cookies?"

"They're there," Brynn said. "But they're for dessert."

"Would you please stop trying to sound like a mother hen?" Chloe said. "And they are *not* here."

She turned and scowled at Phoebe. "Did you eat all those cookies, Blob?"

"Don't be ridiculous," Brynn said. "She's been home sick all day."

"Since when is The Blob ever so sick that she can't inhale a bag of cookies?" Chloe said. "Look, she's all red in the face. She always turns red in the face when she's been caught doing something she shouldn't have."

"Leave her alone, Chloe," Brynn said. "And set the table."

"Can't. I gotta run."

"Run where? It's a school night. Exams are two weeks away. If you don't start studying, Chloe, you're going to fail the year."

"Aw, gee," Chloe said. "Does this mean I won't be able to go to medical school and become a brain surgeon?"

"You think this is all funny, don't you? You want to spend your whole life waiting on tables?"

Chloe stuck out her tongue.

"Set the table."

"I don't have time," Chloe said. "I'm going out. I'll see you later."

"Chloe!" Brynn yelled after her.

But she was already out the door.

* * *

"Where's Shadd?" Chloe asked as soon as she saw Rita. "I thought I was late. How come he isn't here yet?"

Den had a peculiar expression on his face. "He's not coming," he said.

Chloe glanced at Rita and saw that she didn't look right either.

"What's wrong? The cops didn't pick him up, did they?"

"No," Rita said, her voice strained.

"Then what? What's the matter? What's going on?"

Rita glanced over at Den, who smiled in a way that made Chloe's skin crawl.

Rita caught Chloe by the elbow and led her a little way into the park. "Shadd's not coming," she said, "because he's with someone else."

"Someone else?"

Chloe couldn't believe it. After the way he had kissed her on the mountain? And after the way he had kissed her the other day?

"Penny what's-her-name," Rita said. She's in half his classes."

Penny. The girl with the blond hair. The one he'd been talking to in the cafeteria.

"What's he doing with her? Studying?"

Rita shook her head slowly. "Chloe, I heard he asked her to the dance. I think he's interested in her."

"He asked her to the dance?"

It wasn't possible. He couldn't have spent the time he did with Chloe, and then turn around and ask this Penny person to the dance, especially after everything Chloe had done to try to protect him.

132

Nobody could do something as underhanded as that.

"But he's been going out with me," she said.

Rita squeezed her shoulder understandingly. "I know. But I think it has something to do with his father."

"His father? Where does his father come into this?"

"His father's one of those old-fashioned guys. He thinks people should hang around with their own kind."

A knot formed in Chloe's stomach. "What's that supposed to mean?"

"You know," Rita said. Her cheeks turned red and she had trouble keeping her gaze steady on Chloe. "He thinks Shadd should be going out with girls like him."

"White girls, you mean?"

Rita refused to look at her now. Her cheeks were blazing.

"That *is* what you mean, isn't it? His father thinks he should be going out with white girls. And he agrees with his old man. That's what you're telling me."

"Geez, don't shoot the messenger, Chloe. I'm just telling you what happened," Rita said. "You know how some people's parents are. They get unreasonable about stuff like that."

Chloe couldn't believe her ears. "You agree with him too, don't you?"

"I didn't say that," Rita protested.

"But you do."

"You're putting words in my mouth."

"If your father told you he didn't want you going out with a Chinese guy, what would you do?" Chloe asked.

"Don't be silly, Chloe. That would never happen."

"Oh yeah? And why is that? Because you would never want to go out with a Chinese guy in the first place?"

"I didn't say that."

"Well, would you?"

"Would *you?*" Rita said.

"What the hell is that supposed to mean?"

"It's supposed to mean that I don't see you chasing after any Chinese guys yourself. In fact, every time that guy Phil comes around, you run in the opposite direction."

"He's a jerk," Chloe said.

"You sure that's the real reason?"

Chloe glowered at her. What the hell did she mean by that anyway? What did Phil have to do with any of this?

"I don't know why you're mad at me," Rita said. "I didn't do anything."

Chloe sighed. "I know. I'm sorry." She looked at Rita. "You think it's true?"

"That he asked Penny to the dance? I don't know. But it's what I heard."

"So maybe it's not true."

"Maybe," Rita said. But from the look on her face, it didn't seem to Chloe that she was holding out a lot of hope.

"Phoebe, you haven't touched your supper. Are you sure you're okay?"

Phoebe smiled across the table at Brynn. "I'm not hungry."

Brynn stared at her a moment. "Did you eat those cookies?" she said at last.

Reluctantly, Phoebe nodded. They were going to figure it out soon anyway. A whole bag of cookies was missing and she was the only person who had been home all day.

"Geez, Phoebe," Brynn said, shaking her head in annoyance, "when are you going to grow up? A bag of cookies is not a balanced diet."

"I'm sorry." She hung her head. Nothing could make her more ashamed than she already was of what she had done, and Brynn only knew half the story. "I won't do it again." She pushed her chair away from the table. "I'm going to go lie down, okay?"

Brynn shrugged.

Phoebe lay down on her bed and closed her eyes. She hadn't intended to fall asleep, but the next thing she knew, Brynn was shaking her awake.

"There's someone here to see you," she said.

Phoebe frowned as she peered up into her sister's face. Who could it be?

"It's Bobby," Brynn said with a wink. "And you told me you weren't having any luck with guys! It looks to me like you're having luck with this one."

"Bobby? He's here?" It took a few moments for

what Brynn was saying to sink in. This was the first time in Phoebe's life that a boy had come to her house to see her.

"Well come on, Phoebe," Brynn said. "He's not going to stand around all night waiting for you. Do you want to see him or not?"

Phoebe swung her legs over the side of the bed. Did she want to see him? Of course she did. But she looked terrible. She hadn't brushed her hair all day. She had on her oldest, baggiest pair of jeans and a pulled-out-of-shape T-shirt. Her face looked pale and haggard.

"If you want to see him," Brynn said with a smile, "I can tell him to come in and wait for a few minutes. It'll give you time to get changed."

Phoebe gave her sister a grateful glance. Brynn squeezed her arm affectionately.

"Take as much time as you need," she said. "He looks like he'd be ready to wait for an hour if he had to. I think he likes you, Pheeb."

She kept him waiting only fifteen minutes. That's how long it took to pull on a skirt and blouse, rake a brush through her hair, clip on a barrette, and pinch her cheeks hard to get a little colour into them.

Bobby was sitting on the couch in the living room. The TV set was on, but he wasn't watching it. He was looking around the room, as if inspecting it.

Phoebe felt her insides quake. What would he think of their modest apartment? She wondered what his place looked like, whether it was bigger and nicer. Maybe he even lived in a house.

"Hi, Bobby," she said shyly.

He jumped to his feet. "Hi, Phoebe." He just stood there, shifting his gaze from her to the floor and back again. Phoebe waited. After a while he seemed to gather his resolve and he looked her straight in the eye. "So," he said, "I was wondering — "

Brynn walked into the room. Bobby broke off his sentence. His face flushed to a deep scarlet, but Brynn didn't seem to notice.

"You guys okay?" she asked cheerfully. "You want me to make you some lemonade? I think we have a can in the freezer."

"We're fine," Phoebe said. She glanced pointedly at the kitchen.

"Well, okay then," Brynn said. "I guess I'll just mosey off into the kitchen and wash the floor or something." Phoebe watched gratefully as her big sister backed out of the room.

Bobby remained motionless. Then he glanced apprehensively at the kitchen door. "Do you think maybe we could go out?" he said.

"Go out?" Phoebe's heart began to pound. Did he mean, like, go steady?

"Outside," he said. "You know, where we could kind of be alone. Maybe we could take a walk."

"Oh." She told herself she was being silly. Why would he want to go out with her? But still, he had come to see her. And he'd brought her flowers at the hospital. He wouldn't have done that if he didn't at least like her. "Sure," she said. "We could go over to the park."

"Do you have to tell your sister or anything?"

Phoebe shook her head. "I'm not a kid," she said. "I can take care of myself."

* * *

"Hi, guys."

Chloe whirled around. "Shadd!"

She was glad now that she hadn't believed what Rita had said about Shadd being with Penny. Obviously Rita had got it all wrong. Rita never seemed to have a very clear idea of what was going on around her. She got everything wrong.

"I figured I'd find you two up here." Shadd sat down on the grass near Chloe, Den and Rita, and stretched out his legs.

"What happened?" Den asked. He was sucking on a stalk of long grass. "Penny's old man tell you to get lost?"

Chloe glanced sharply at Den. "Why don't you just shut up for a change?" she said. "You don't even know what's going on."

"*I* don't know what's going on?" Den said. He laughed drily. "That's a good one."

"Pig," Chloe said under her breath.

"Hey, come on," Shadd said, "let's be friends. Why don't you two just cool it and we can all enjoy the evening?"

"So it's not true, right?" Chloe said.

"What's not true?"

"Rita said that you asked Penny what's-her-name to the dance. That's not true, is it?"

His look was so calm that she knew instantly that it was true.

"It depends how you look at it," he said slowly. "It's no big deal."

"Oh, yes it is," Chloe said. She punched him hard on the arm. "You rat. You've been leading me on the whole time, haven't you?"

"Hey," Shadd protested. "That hurt."

Chloe got to her feet. "You're a real creep, you know that? You've been going around with me for a couple of weeks and now, a couple of days before the biggest dance of the whole year, you ask Penny to go with you." She felt like kicking him hard. Instead she turned to leave.

"Hey, come on, Chloe," Shadd said. He was on his feet and had caught her by the arm. "It's all a matter of how you look at it."

Chloe glowered at him. "Are you going to the dance with her or not?"

He nodded slowly. "But only because I promised her first."

"You what?"

"I went out with her before I started kind of going out with you."

Chloe glanced at Rita. Rita shrugged. Neither of them had known that.

"I promised her a month ago that I'd go to the dance with her."

"But you don't go with her any more. You go with me."

"I know," Shadd said. "And I know it doesn't seem fair. But a promise is a promise. She was in such bad shape when we broke up . . ."

"She didn't look in such bad shape the other day when I saw you in the cafeteria with her."

"She doesn't mean anything to me," Shadd said. He held Chloe's arms and peered into her eyes. "I'm just taking her to the dance, and that's it."

"Take her to the dance, take her to the moon, take her any place you want, I don't care. We're through."

Fear flickered in his eyes. "Wait, Chloe, don't say that."

"Why not? You don't care about me. If you did, you'd be taking me to the dance, not some old girlfriend."

"But Chloe — "

"Don't touch me! I mean it, Shadd. I thought you cared about me, and it turns out you don't at all. And after everything I did for you. Geez, I lied to the cops for you. Am I ever sorry I did that!" The worried look on Shadd's face deepened.

"What's that supposed to mean?" he asked.

"Yeah," Den said. "What's that supposed to mean?"

"Butt out, Den. This is none of your business," Chloe said.

"Wrong," Den said. "It's all of our business now. We were all there when it happened and we all told the cops the same story. If you do anything stupid now, we're all going to get into trouble."

"Oh my God," Rita moaned.

"Shut up, Rita," Chloe said. "I didn't say I was going to do anything. I'm just sorry I tried to help him in the first place." She turned back to Shadd. "I don't believe your stupid story about Penny. I don't think you're taking her because of what you told her a month ago. I think you have other reasons for wanting to take her."

"Chloe . . . " Rita said.

Shadd glanced over his shoulder at her. "What did you say to her, Rita?"

"The truth," Den said. "What your old man would say if you ever brought home a Chinese chick."

Shadd's face deepened in colour. He turned slowly back to Chloe. "That has nothing to do with this, Chloe."

"Right," Chloe said. "I bet."

She turned and walked away alone down the mountain.

chapter 14

Phoebe flew at her almost the moment she stepped into the apartment.

"Guess what, Chloe," she said as she danced around in front of her sister. "Guess what happened to me."

"You swallowed a basketball and that's why you're such a blob," Chloe said irritably.

This time, Phoebe did not start shrieking at her. Nor did she burst into tears. "I have a date for the prom," she said. "I'm going to the dance."

"What happened?" Chloe said. "Did a blind kid move into the neighbourhood?"

Phoebe stuck out her tongue. "I don't care what you say," she said. "I have a date for the prom."

"What are you going to wear?"

Phoebe's smile faded.

"You don't have anything to wear, do you?" Chloe smiled. "Could be interesting. Maybe you'll set a new style for proms. Sweatshirt chic."

Chloe saw tears gathering in the corners of Phoebe's eyes, but Phoebe managed to keep a check on them.

"Leave her alone, why don't you?" said Brynn as she stepped into the hall. "What's the matter with you?"

"Nothing." Chloe steered a path between her sisters.

"Someone's here to see you," Brynn called after her.

Chloe turned back expectantly. "Shadd?"

"Lieutenant Levesque."

"He wants to see me? What about?"

Brynn shrugged. "He just said he wanted to see you. He's in the kitchen, having a cup of coffee."

"Where's Mom?"

"Working."

Chloe squared her shoulders. What did Levesque want? She knew for a fact that Den and Rita had told the cops the same story that she had. There was no way the cops could have connected Shadd with what happened, and if that was true, there was no way they could connect her, either.

The big police detective was seated at the kitchen table, one huge hand wrapped around a pottery mug from which steam rose. He looked up and smiled when Chloe entered the room.

"I've been waiting for you," he said.

"I know. Brynn told me. What do you want?"

She brushed casually by him and opened the cupboard above the sink. She pulled down a glass and then rummaged in the fridge for a soda. He didn't say anything until after she had sat down with her drink.

"It's about the incident with the old man," he said.

"I already told you I don't know anything about that."

"I believe you also told me that there aren't very

143

many Asian girls in your school."

She nodded.

He reached down under the table and picked up a brown paper bag. From it he pulled out a red wool sweater, which he unfolded and spread onto the table.

"Do you know anyone who has a sweater like this?"

Chloe's heart leapt to her throat. She recognized the sweater immediately. It was a struggle to keep her face impassive and her voice calm.

"A red sweater?" she said. "There must be a million of those in a city this size."

"True," Levesque said. "But not all red sweaters are alike. This one, for instance, wasn't bought at a department store. It was bought at a small boutique down on Crescent Street."

"So?" Chloe said.

"So sometimes it's possible to find out who bought a sweater like this in a small store because in a small store they tend to keep more detailed sales records."

Keep calm, Chloe told herself. Don't panic. "So did you find out who bought that one?"

Levesque shook his head. "Unfortunately, no," he said. "Perhaps you'd like to take a closer look at it."

"Me?" Chloe stared at him. "Why would I want to look at it? I'm not a cop."

"But you are missing a red sweater, aren't you?" he said. Panic surged through Chloe, and suddenly she was no longer confident that she could keep the emotion from her face.

"No, I'm not."

Levesque scratched his chin thoughtfully. "That's funny," he went on. "I was certain your sister mentioned that you tore the place apart the other day, looking for a red sweater."

"I found it."

"I see." Levesque carefully folded the red sweater on the table and slipped it back into its bag. "May I see your sweater?"

"No, you may not," Chloe replied. "It's not here."

"Where is it?"

"I loaned it to a friend of mine."

"Your friend Rita perhaps?"

Chloe forced herself to take a sip of the soda she no longer wanted. If she said Rita had the sweater, maybe he would go over there and demand to see it. And if Rita was unable to produce it . . .

"Well, never mind," Levesque said. He set the bag and the sweater onto the floor at his feet again. "There is something that I need your help with, though. An imposition, I realize, but I'm afraid it's the only way we can think of to get to the bottom of this case."

Chloe took another sip.

"We did what you suggested," Levesque said.

"What I suggested?"

"We went to the principal of your school and obtained a list of all the Asian girls attending Earl Barron. As you said, there aren't very many. We're going to get them all together tomorrow and let the old man see if he recognizes any of them. I wonder if you would mind participating?"

"Me? I already told you. I didn't have anything to do with what happened to any old man. I wasn't anywhere near any old man when it happened."

"You did tell me that," Levesque agreed. "But the way a police line-up works, we have to have enough people similar to the one the victim has described so that it really is an exercise in identification. Since you fit the description we were given and you do live in the neighbourhood . . . "

"Do I have any choice?" Chloe asked.

He didn't answer.

Chloe sank onto the chair opposite him and stared down into her glass. Ever since the beginning she had had the feeling that something like this was going to happen. Now that it finally had, she wasn't sure how she felt. A little afraid, that was for sure. But also a little relieved.

"Can I tell you something?" she said slowly, looking right into his dark eyes.

Levesque leaned across the table toward her. "Sure," he said. "If you have something to say, I'll listen."

* * *

"Did you hear what happened last night?" Edie said the next morning.

Brynn stared at her in astonishment. Surely it wasn't all over town already? "Of course I heard," she said. "But I'm surprised that you did."

Edie frowned. "What are you talking about?"

"What are *you* talking about?" Brynn asked.

"Mickey."

"Mickey?"

"Mickey Shea. He called me up last night."

"That's great," Brynn said with all the enthusiasm she could muster. It wasn't much. Things had been in such an uproar the previous night. When her mother had heard about what happened in that Chinese restaurant, she'd yelled at Chloe and grounded her for the whole summer. Brynn doubted the grounding would last, though. Having Chloe moping around the place for more than a day would drive everyone so crazy that their mother would probably end up kicking her out of the apartment.

"Hey, what's the matter with you?" Edie asked. "I thought you'd be happy for me."

"I am," Brynn said. "I'm very happy for you, Edie. Aren't I the one who told you that Mickey had a thing for you in the first place?"

Edie giggled. "You were right because, guess what?"

"What?"

"Brynn, you're supposed to guess."

"He asked you to marry him."

"Very funny," Edie said. "You're supposed to make a serious guess."

"He declared his undying love for you."

"Brynn! Come on."

"What then?"

Edie's smile was so broad it split her face in half.

"He asked me to the dance."

Brynn stared at her. "To the spring dance?"

Edie nodded. "He was so nice about it, too. He told me he'd had his eye on me for a while, but that he knew I was going out with Evan. Then he said after I broke up with Evan, he wasn't sure whether to ask me or not, you know, because he thought I might be upset. He's such a sweet guy. You know what, Brynn? I think I'm in love again."

"Great," said Brynn. She forced herself to sound happy. But all she could see in her mind was Evan, sitting in the shade of the schoolyard with Angeline. It wasn't fair. If Mickey Shea had only asked Edie out a few days earlier, it could have been Brynn sitting there with Evan instead.

Edie looked upset. "You're not mad at me, are you?" she said.

"Mad?"

"I know we made all those plans for the night of the dance. But you understand, don't you, Brynn? I really like Mickey. He's such a sweet guy. And you know if it was the other way around, if you suddenly fell head over heels in love the way I just have, that I wouldn't stand in your way. So you don't mind, do you, Brynn?"

"No," Brynn said. "I don't mind."

Anyway, it was too late.

* * *

"What about this one?" Cindy said, holding up a dress on a hanger. "It's kind of nice."

It was grey, with buttons down the front and lace

at the collar. It looked like it belonged in an old woman's closet. "It's too old-fashioned," Phoebe said.

"But the price is right," Cindy said. She held out the tag. "It's the nicest thing we've seen for the money you can spend, Pheeb."

"I am not wearing that dress. I'd rather wear nothing at all."

"You may have to," Cindy said. "This is the last thrift shop in the area. If you don't find something here, you'll have to go naked."

Phoebe sighed and ran her hand along the rack of dresses. It was true. They'd had no luck at all at either the Salvation Army or the St. Vincent de Paul. If she didn't unearth something here, she didn't know what she was going to do.

"Hey," Cindy said excitedly. Then her mood switched abruptly as she looked inside the garment she was holding. "Aw," she said. "It's too small."

Phoebe was transfixed by the dress Cindy held in her hand. It was the most beautiful dress she had ever seen — deep blue, like the Mediterranean on a picture postcard, with sequins that glistened in the afternoon sun streaming through the window. At the top were two tiny spaghetti straps.

"How much is it?" she said.

Cindy glanced at the tag. "More than you have," she said. "And besides, Pheeb, it's not your size."

Phoebe wasn't listening. She slipped the dress off Cindy's arm and onto her own and ran her hand over its shimmering surface.

"It would be nice, wouldn't it?" she said longingly. "You know what's going to happen. One of those skinny girls is going to find it and wear it. I just know it." She caught the dress tag between her fingers and stared at it. It was only one size too small.

"How much money do you have on you, Cindy?"

"But, Phoebe, it's too small."

"How much?" Phoebe demanded.

Cindy pulled her wallet from her purse and slowly counted its contents. "Six dollars and thirty cents."

"Lend me five and I'll have enough."

"But, Phoebe, I still have to buy some eye shadow and some mascara, and I wanted to get some pantyhose . . ."

"I'll pay you back as soon as I get home. Brynn will lend me the money. She's not going to the dance."

"But it won't fit," Cindy said.

Phoebe looked down at the dress again. "Yes it will," she said. "I'm going to make it fit."

chapter 15

"Get away from me," Rita said. She slammed her locker shut. "Get away from me and stay away from me. I can't believe you did what you did. It was bad enough when the cops wanted to talk to me that first time. My mother got so weak in the knees she almost fainted. When they turned up the second time, my parents totally freaked out. I'm grounded for a month. And I'm not allowed to go to the dance. And it's all your fault."

"Rita, I didn't have any choice."

"What are you talking about? Of course you had a choice. You were just mad at Shadd, so you decided to get revenge. Only you didn't stop to think what that was going to do to the rest of us. Den's in trouble too. His father went through the roof when he found out what happened. And I heard that Shadd's been suspended. He might even get expelled."

"The cops had my red sweater, Rita. The one I lost the night it happened. They were going to put me in a line-up."

Rita's eyes widened.

"What?"

"They knew I was one of the girls involved. An Asian girl." It figured that it had worked against her. It hadn't ever worked for her.

"You mean you wouldn't have told them otherwise?"

Chloe shrugged. She had been wondering the same thing herself. "I don't know. I didn't have the chance to find out. And I got grounded. At least until we go to court on it."

"My mother's going to kill me if it turns out some judge says we did something wrong."

"We should have stayed around to help the guy," Chloe said. "What if he'd been badly hurt?"

"He wasn't," Rita said.

"You think Shadd will ever speak to me again?"

Rita shrugged, then shook her head slowly. "He's pretty mad. So's Den. He told me he doesn't want me hanging around with you."

Chloe gazed evenly into Rita's eyes. "So what're you going to do?"

Rita shrugged. Then she flashed an impish smile. "What are you doing the night of the dance?" she said. "Maybe we could talk our moms into letting you come over to my place, just for the one night. I know if I cry enough, I can get my mother at least talking to your mother." She slipped an arm around Chloe and giggled. A smile spread slowly across Chloe's face.

* * *

It was getting so easy, Phoebe almost didn't have to think about it. She kept a handful of SlimNows in her pocket and ate half of one, washing it down with a mouthful of hot water from the tap, every hour or two. She got up earlier than everyone else so that she could say she had already eaten her breakfast. Instead of going to the cafeteria at lunchtime, she went to the gym and ran laps, and she kept going past the point when she thought she was going to drop. She ran again after school, then sat in the park with a cup of hot tea and a SlimNow. When she finally did go home, well past seven, she told Brynn she had been studying at Cindy's and had had supper there. She was sorry, she told her, that she had forgotten to call.

After a while, she didn't feel hungry at all. That was the funny part. She had spent almost her whole life being hungry — craving peanut butter or chocolate, or lying on her bed late on Sunday afternoon, mouth watering while a roast chicken or a roast of pork baked in the oven. Sunday was still her favourite day. Her mother was usually home on Sunday, and she always made a special dinner with some pie or a cake or pastries for dessert, with ice cream on the side. The roast chicken Sundays were the best, because Phoebe loved bread stuffing smothered in chicken gravy. It was her favourite food of all. She would be glad when the prom was finally over. Then maybe she could stop inventing excuses for not being home for Sunday dinner.

Maybe then she could treat herself to something special too. A chocolate éclair from the Viennese bakery on Sherbrooke Street. Or maybe a *mille feuilles*, the thin layers of pastry sandwiching rich custard and real whipped cream, the sugar icing on top thick and creamy.

But for now she sipped her tea and nibbled on pieces of SlimNow. And when she woke up in the middle of the night after a dream of food, all she had to do was turn on the light and open her closet door and gaze at the blue sequined dress and think about what it would be like to put that dress on and walk into the Earl Barron gymnasium with Bobby Keough.

* * *

Chloe turned the corner and felt as if she had walked straight into a brick wall. There stood Philomen, only a short distance away from her, straining to get a stack of books to stay put on the top shelf of his locker.

Philomen was the last person she wanted to see. She took a step backward, hoping to duck back around the corner. But it was too late. He looked away from his locker and directly at her. He didn't look like his usually cheery self. In fact, he wasn't smiling at all.

Chloe pulled herself up straight. Earl Barron was a big school, but it wasn't so big that you could avoid someone indefinitely — especially when he was in three of your classes. Besides, she told herself, she had done the right thing. She'd told the cops the whole story, even if it had taken her a little while to get around to it. She had even apologized to the old man — her mother had insisted on it. She was sure Philomen knew the whole story by now. Besides, she didn't actually have to talk to him. All she had to do was walk down the hallway past him.

She started toward him slowly, to prove to him

she wasn't afraid. But the closer she got to him, the quicker her pace became.

"Hello, Chloe," he said softly when she drew even with him.

"Hiya, Phil." She kept her voice light and her eyes straight ahead.

"Chloe . . . "

His voice was the faintest whisper. She couldn't keep herself from turning to face him.

"There is a dance this Saturday night," he said.

Her first reaction was to laugh, but she knew he wouldn't understand why she was doing it, so she confined herself to a smile.

"I know," she said. "Are you going?"

Philomen's cheeks grew as red as cherries. "I was thinking . . . I was going to ask you to the dance."

"Me?" She couldn't believe her ears. "After what happened to your grandfather, you want to ask me to the dance?"

"You said it was an accident," Philomen said.

"And you believe me?"

His smooth face clouded. "Should I not believe you?"

"Well, yeah," Chloe said. "Yeah, you should believe me." She felt embarrassed. She had always thought Phil was kind of a jerk. He certainly wasn't acting in a normal way now. But he seemed so sincere. "Don't get me wrong. I told the police the truth. But a lot of people wouldn't believe me, you know?"

He shook his head.

"Look, Phil . . . " she began.

Something on the top shelf of his locker suddenly gave way. Books, notepaper, pencils, a geometry set all cascaded down onto his head, and came to rest around his feet.

"You okay?" Chloe asked.

His algebra text had bounced off the top of his head. "I am fine," he said, rubbing his scalp. "I have too many things in my locker."

"I know what you mean," Chloe said. She bent down to help pick up his belongings. "My locker's a bit of a mess too. There's stuff in the back of it that I haven't seen since September."

Philomen kneeled down beside her and started to stack his books.

"Hey," Chloe said. She reached for something half hidden under the cover of a history text. "Hey, what's this?"

She held up a heart-shaped pin and slowly turned it over. Three pink roses were painted on the front of the heart, their stems twining around the sides. In the middle, in elegant script, were the initials *C.Y.*

"Where did you get this?" Chloe asked.

Philomen stared at the pin. Then he looked at Chloe.

* * *

Brynn leaned back against the cool concrete of the statue and pulled her knees up to her chest. Edie had invited her to go dress shopping, but Brynn didn't feel up to it. Instead she had walked down to the playing field and settled herself in the shade to watch the baseball game. Evan was playing second base. He hadn't noticed her, and she told herself she didn't care. Angeline was sitting over near the mesh backstop. She smiled over at Evan every few minutes.

A shadow fell across Brynn's legs. She shaded her eyes with her hand and squinted up to see who was there.

"You like baseball?" Levesque said.

Brynn shrugged. "It's okay, I guess," she said. "Mostly I like to sit outside."

"And watch the boys, eh?" Levesque said with a smile. He peered across the field, and it seemed to Brynn that his eyes rested on Evan. "That young man over there, the one in the red T-shirt, is he the one you have your eye on?"

Brynn felt her face burning straight to the roots of her hair. "I don't have my eye on anyone," she said.

Levesque sat down next to her and pulled up a stalk of long grass to chew on. "There's a big dance at Earl Barron this Saturday," he said. "I saw posters all over the school when I was there."

Brynn nodded but didn't look at him. She wasn't even sure how she felt about him after the whole thing with Chloe — although it was true that if he hadn't been around to calm down the situation, her mother might have up and shipped Chloe off to a school for problem kids. Brynn wasn't sure how she felt about that, either. Sometimes it seemed to her that maximum discipline would be a good thing for Chloe.

"Are you going?" he said.

"Going where?"

"To the dance on Saturday."

Brynn shook her head. "I have too much else to do," she said. "Exams are coming up in a couple of weeks."

Levesque nodded and chewed on his stalk of grass a few moments longer. "Well, I have some work to do. I guess I'd better be going," he said at last, much to Brynn's relief.

Brynn nodded, but said nothing.

"I'll see you later," he said. "Your mother has invited me over for dinner."

Brynn stared at him in astonishment. She couldn't remember the last time her mother had invited a man to supper. Nor, she realized, could she remember the last time any man her mother had gone out with had shown much interest in her kids.

"Is something wrong?" Levesque asked.

"She . . . she isn't a very good cook," Brynn said. It wasn't exactly true, but it was the first thing that popped into her mind.

Levesque shrugged. "Nobody's perfect."

Brynn hesitated before asking, "Do you like my mother?"

Levesque smiled. "I do," he said. "I like her very much. In fact, I like the whole family."

* * *

"If you want to do the dishes, that's fine," Chloe said. "If you want to ask for volunteers to help you do the dishes, that's fine too. But I don't like being drafted. You could have got Brynn to help you."

"Brynn helped your mother make the dinner," said Levesque. "I thought the least we could do was clean up."

Chloe heard someone knocking on the front door. She started out of the kitchen to answer it, but Levesque tossed her a dishtowel.

"I'm sure someone else will get that," he said.

Sure enough, she heard the door open and the distant exchange of voices. Then, "Chloe!" It was Brynn calling her. "Chloe, there's someone here to see you."

Please let it be Shadd, she thought. She hadn't seen him since she had talked to the police. She tossed the dishtowel back to Levesque.

"Feel free to start without me," she said.

"I'll wait until you get back."

Chloe made a sour face.

"Who is it?" she whispered to Brynn as she passed through the living room.

"A guy."

"What guy?"

"An Asian guy."

Chloe groaned. Not Phil. Not again.

She stepped out onto the outside landing and pulled the door shut behind her. "Hiya, Phil," she said. She wished he would just go away.

"Hello, Chloe."

He smiled shyly, and that irritated her more than his presence.

"I want to explain to you — "

"I don't want to hear it, Phil."

"But you are angry."

"You bet I'm angry," Chloe said. "I don't understand what kind of stupid game you were playing. You knew all along that that pin and sweater belonged to me, didn't you? What were you going to do, blackmail me into going to the dance with you? Well, you can forget it. Even if I wasn't grounded, I wouldn't go with you. So why don't you just run along. I'm sure your grandfather can use some help down at the restaurant."

She didn't wait to see what he was going to do or say. She turned, went inside, closed the door behind her, and prayed that he wouldn't knock and insist on speaking to her again.

"What did he want?" Brynn asked as Chloe stormed through the living room on her way back to the kitchen.

"Nothing. He didn't want anything."

She grabbed the dishtowel out of Levesque's hand. He plunged his hands into the soapy water and began to wash the dishes. "Boy trouble?" he asked.

"Geek trouble," Chloe said irritably. "This guy just won't leave me alone."

"Maybe he likes you."

"That would be just my luck. All the wrong people fall head over heels in love with me."

"Is that so?" Levesque said. "What's wrong with this one? Is he irresponsible?"

"Philomen?" Chloe rolled her eyes. "This guy's more responsible than the prime minister."

"Does he have bad breath? A bad complexion? Is he mean? Does he pick on younger kids?"

"Well, no," Chloe said. "But he wears white gym socks for all occasions. And he's always the first to put his hand up in class. And it's hard to understand what he's saying."

"And that's why you don't like him?"

"No, of course not," Chloe said. It was, though. Well, sort of. But now that she'd said all those things out loud, she realized how shallow she would sound if she admitted that they were the reasons she didn't like him.

"Philomen," Levesque said. "That's a very unusual name. Doesn't that old man have a grandson named Philomen?"

"It's the same guy," Chloe said. She was pretty sure that Levesque knew already. He seemed to know everything else.

"I spoke to him," Levesque said. Of course, Chloe thought. "He seems like a nice boy."

"Sure," Chloe said. "If you like the type."

"And what type is that?"

"The geek type."

"Oh." Levesque rinsed a glass under clear water and set it into the dish drainer. "For a moment I thought perhaps you meant something else."

"Yeah? What?"

161

He shrugged. "I thought maybe because he's Chinese . . . "

Chloe glared at him. "That's really smart," she said. "I can see where you'd be a top-notch investigator. In case you haven't noticed, I'm Chinese, too. At least, half of me is."

"I know," Levesque said. "That's why I'm confused. He seems like a nice kid."

"I'm not interested in him," Chloe said. "Besides, even if I wanted to go to the dance with him, which I don't, I'm grounded for the foreseeable future."

"You're grounded until you have your court date," Levesque corrected her.

"I can't believe I even got charged. I didn't do anything."

"You lied to the police. That's a criminal offense."

"People lie to the police all the time. Do they all end up getting charged?"

Levesque shrugged. "Maybe someone decided you needed to learn a lesson."

"Someone?"

"You have a court appearance tomorrow."

"Tomorrow? So soon? I thought it was going to take longer."

Levesque shrugged. "I thought maybe you'd prefer to get it over with."

"What do you think is going to happen?" Chloe asked. "Are they going to send me to some institution?"

Levesque swooshed water over a handful of cutlery and dropped it into the drainer. "I doubt it. You haven't been in any trouble before. Not with the law, anyway. But running away like that and lying to the police, those things are serious. From what I understand, your case worker is going to suggest some kind of community service."

"Community service?"

"Instead of a fine or some other punishment, the judge can sentence people to undertake a task that serves the community. Some people have to work so many hours in a seniors' home, or in a hospital or a community centre."

"I'm going to work in an old folks' home?" The thought made Chloe shudder.

"Actually," Levesque said, "what I heard was that they're going to recommend that you and your friend Rita work at the old man's restaurant. That way both sides can get to know each other. I think you'll find it very educational."

Chloe groaned. Why me? she thought.

chapter 16

It was one of those days. Edie draped herself over Mickey and stayed that way most of the day. She had a big, goofy grin on her face and a faraway look in her eyes, like she was imagining a perfect future with Mickey. Angeline Phillips draped herself over Evan. Her grin had a sharp edge to it and there was nothing dreamlike in the way she smirked at Brynn. Embarrassed, Brynn looked away.

In chemistry lab, Brynn made a point of keeping her eyes on the blackboard. It wasn't easy. Evan sat directly in front of her, and he kept twisting his head around. She didn't presume to think that he was looking at her. Angeline was sitting two benches behind her.

Brynn heard a gentle *pssst*. It sounded as though it was coming from Evan, but she didn't look at him. After all, he wasn't trying to attract her attention. It was Angeline he was interested in. Then a wadded up scrap of paper fell onto the open binder in front of Brynn. She glanced around, wondering where it had come from. Her eyes met Evan's. He grinned at her. Quickly, she looked away.

She fingered the ball of paper, then, after checking to ensure that no one was watching her, she gently smoothed it out. *Can I talk to you after class?* it said.

Angrily she scrunched it up and, without thinking, turned around and lobbed it at Angeline.

"Miss Laurendeau," Mr. Moffat, the chemistry teacher, said, "precisely what do you think you're doing?"

Brynn's face burned.

"She threw something at me, sir," Angeline said.

Mr. Moffat placed his hands on his hips. "Miss Laurendeau, will you please stand?"

Brynn stumbled to her feet, but kept her eyes firmly focussed on the tabletop. This was so humiliating.

"Would you care to tell me the reason for this disruption?" Mr. Moffat said. "Are you finding chemistry a little boring? Do you feel the need to throw things in order to liven it up?"

"No, sir," Brynn murmured.

"Speak up," Mr. Moffat said. "We can't hear you, can we, people?"

If a fairy godmother had offered Brynn one wish at that moment, she would have chosen invisibility.

"Miss Laurendeau?"

"Yes, sir? I mean, no, sir." Then, afraid he hadn't heard, she said again, in a much louder voice, "No, sir."

"Thank you, Miss Laurendeau. Now would you be so kind as to take your seat, and refrain from launching missiles at your fellow students for the remainder of this class?"

"Yes, sir," Brynn said. She was only too happy to reclaim her seat and to scrunch herself down into as tiny a ball as she could manage.

Not more than five minutes had passed before another paper ball landed on her desk. Without even glancing at it, she swept it onto the floor. How dare he continue his stupid little game with Angeline after he had already gotten her into trouble once? She heard it again. *Pssst.*

She refused to even glance at him. If he had a message for Angeline, let him deliver it himself. She wasn't going to help him.

"*Pssst.* Brynn."

He could drop dead for all she cared.

"Brynn."

It was what her mother would have called a stage whisper, so loud that everyone in the class could hear it. Brynn froze as Mr. Moffat turned away from the blackboard and fixed her with his iciest stare.

"Miss Laurendeau, are you creating another disturbance in my classroom?"

Brynn glared at Evan. How dare he get her into more trouble?

"Well?"

Brynn cleared her throat and started to stand again to face yet more humiliation. Then, suddenly, Evan was on his feet in front of her.

"It wasn't Brynn," he said.

"Indeed," Mr. Moffat said. "Then who was it?"

"It was me."

"You?" Mr. Moffat inspected him as if he were examining a new species of cockroach. "And pray,

Mr. O'Neill, why were you disrupting my class?"

Unlike Brynn, Evan did not seem at all embarrassed. He held himself straight, looked Mr. Moffat in the eye, and said, "I was trying to get Brynn's attention."

From somewhere near the back of the room, Brynn heard a small gasp. A couple of other girls giggled. Mr. Moffat's face grew even more sombre.

"Might I suggest, Mr. O'Neill, that you have succeeded in your mission. Indeed, you have surpassed your goal. You have succeeded in getting not only Miss Laurendeau's attention, but mine and the rest of the class's as well. If only you were succeeding as well in your chemistry studies."

Several people laughed this time.

"Since you seem in no further need of instruction for the day, may I suggest that you stretch your legs by taking a walk down to the office to see Mr. Rusnek? You may take Miss Laurendeau with you."

Brynn stared in astonishment at the chemistry teacher.

"Now, Miss Laurendeau," he said.

She gathered her books in silence and walked from the room ahead of Evan. She heard the squeak of his sneakers behind her and quickened her pace.

"Hey," he said, "wait up."

She moved as fast as she could without actually running.

"If you don't stop," he said behind her, "I'll yell and we'll both end up in detention."

She came to a halt and turned to face him. "Haven't you got me into enough trouble for one day?"

"Me? You're the one who started it. The way you lobbed that note at Angeline, you looked like you wished it was a rock."

"You started it," Brynn said. "I'm not a relay station. The next time you have a note for somebody, deliver it yourself."

Evan frowned. "What are you talking about? I did deliver it myself. That message was for *you*, Brynn."

"It was not." It couldn't be. Why would it be?

"I dropped it on your desk, didn't I? The way you've been ducking me every time I come down the hall, I haven't gotten close enough to talk to you. I thought maybe a note . . . "

"You want to talk to me?" She regarded him with suspicion. "What about?"

"About the dance," he said. "Look, I know it's late, and I know you must have told me a million times already that you weren't interested, but you know me. Never-say-die O'Neill. I thought it couldn't hurt to ask one more time . . . "

"Ask what? What are you talking about?"

"The dance. I want to know if you'll go to the dance with me tomorrow night, Brynn."

* * *

It was one of those days. Phoebe drifted down the hallway at school feeling as insubstantial as a butterfly. She had lost weight. It hardly seemed possible, but she had done it. She had stepped off the bathroom scale with a big grin on her face the night before, after staring in disbelief at the numbers hovering under the red line. And even though the evidence had been right before her eyes, her hands had trembled when she plucked the sequined dress from her closet and gently pulled down the zipper.

She stepped into the dress and pulled it carefully up over her hips. The silky lining glided over her body. True, she had to hold her tummy in a little to get the zipper closed. But she was confident that fasting for the rest of the day and then all day tomorrow would solve the problem.

Phoebe kept her eyes averted from the mirror, and stepped back far enough from it that her whole body would be visible from head to toe when she looked into it again.

Then she hesitated. What if the dress looked terrible on her? What if it just made her look ridiculous? She wouldn't have time to find a substitute and, besides, she didn't have any more money.

Slowly she raised her eyes — and stifled a small gasp. The dress was wonderful — like a sheet of sapphire wrapped around her body. The fabric was sleek against her skin; the sequins caught the light and danced in it. The dress fit. It made her look . . . almost beautiful.

Phoebe sailed through the day like a kite on the breeze, floating and soaring, picturing how great she had looked in the dress. Tomorrow night, when she slipped the dress back on and walked into the gymnasium with Bobby Keough, she would be a princess-in-waiting, a Cinderella gone to the ball.

* * *

It was one of those days. Rita's mother dabbed at her tears all the way through the hearing. Rita's father sat beside her, stiff-backed and stern-faced. A few seats over from them was Den's mother. While she listened to the proceedings, she twisted the straw handle of her handbag. Shadd's father sat right up in the front row, where he could scowl at the lawyers, the judge and Chloe. Chloe found it hard to relate his sour-looking face to Shadd's care-free, handsome one. She wondered if Shadd would look more like his father as he grew older.

Chloe's mother sat stiffly in her chair, flanked on one side by Levesque, who had worked hard all the way down to the courthouse, trying to convince her that Chloe was in no danger of ending up in custody. Now the judge was sentencing her to something worse. She had to work Friday nights and Saturdays for six weeks at the old man's restaurant.

"Cheer up," Levesque said when the hearing was over. "It could have been a lot worse."

"But he probably hates me already. I can just imagine what he's going to make me do."

"If he does hate you," Levesque said, "which I doubt, it's because he hasn't had the opportunity to get to know you the way I have."

He smiled, but Chloe couldn't decide if he was

serious or if he was pulling her leg. She glanced over at the old man who had sat silently through the proceedings. Every now and then his lawyer had leaned across him to whisper to a younger Chinese man. Then the younger Chinese man had whispered into the old man's ear. Chloe decided that the younger man was making sure Philomen's grandfather understood everything that was going on. At the point when the judge sentenced Rita and Chloe, the old man smiled grimly.

Den and Shadd received a different sentence. They were to work as volunteers on weekends at a local hospital. And the judge told Shadd that if he ever appeared in court again for any reason, he'd be spending a lot of time away from home.

Chloe stole a glance at Shadd. He met her gaze. He didn't look angry, but that wasn't much comfort. She was stung by his seeming indifference to her now. He hadn't spoken to her since she had told Levesque everything that had happened. Chloe breathed a sigh of relief when the hearing was finally adjourned. All she wanted was to get out of the courthouse, get home, and concentrate on being as sweet as she could to her mother so that, with luck, she wouldn't be grounded for the whole summer. Two months of staring at the four walls of her bedroom would just about drive her crazy.

She started down the aisle behind her mother and Levesque, and was surprised when a hand reached out and grabbed her. She looked into Shadd's father's grey eyes.

"You know what the trouble is with you people?" he said angrily.

What was his problem? "What people are you talking about, Mr. Meadowcroft?" she said.

"You foreigners," he said. "You come here and you don't want to learn to get along like everyone else. You're thick as thieves, always keeping to yourselves, always thinking you're better than everyone else."

His vehemence astonished Chloe.

"I'm not a foreigner," she said, trembling a little. "I was born here, just like you. And I bet I get along a whole lot better than people like you." She started to move past Shadd's father, but he blocked her. Levesque tapped him on the shoulder and showed his badge.

"Is there a problem?" he said.

Mr. Meadowcroft didn't answer. He continued to scowl at Chloe, but he stepped aside to let her pass. Chloe walked out of the courtroom without looking back.

chapter 17

Brynn brushed frantically at her hair, but the effect was worse, not better. As she studied the results in her mirror, she despaired of ever being ready for Evan.

She'd never paid much attention to her hair before. It had always gone perfectly well with her clothes. She had been dismayed to discover, however, that it did not go perfectly well with the slim green dress that her mother had produced for her out of the back of her closet.

"I've had it for years, but it never goes out of style," her mother said. "I used to wear it to go dancing with your father. It'll look beautiful on you, honey."

In fact, it looked positively startling. Brynn had to take a second look in the mirror to assure herself that the grown-up body she was looking at was really her own. Her hair, however, was another matter. Limp and unruly, it most definitely belonged to her.

"You can't beat it into submission, you know," said a softly sarcastic voice behind her. Brynn turned and saw Chloe leaning against the doorframe, watching her.

"I've tried everything," Brynn moaned. "Nothing helps. I should never have started fooling with it in the first place. I should have left it the way it was."

"Wrong," Chloe said firmly. "It's about time you did something with your hair. You just have to know what you're doing."

"Well, I don't."

"Want some help?"

Brynn stared at her sister. "Don't tell me you're actually volunteering to help me?"

Chloe shrugged. "Why not? I'm going nuts around here with nothing to do." She took the brush from Brynn's hand and told her to sit down. "What a switch, huh? You and The Blob are going to dances, and I have to go over to that restaurant and mop floors all night. Now I know what Cinderella felt like."

Brynn arched an eyebrow. "Are you calling me an ugly step-sister?"

Chloe laughed. "By the time I get finished with you, everyone's going to think you're Cinderella." She hummed to herself as she started to work on Brynn's hair.

Brynn heard someone at the front door, and immediately leaped up from her chair. "Don't tell me that's Evan already!"

"Relax," Chloe said. "It's still early. It's probably just Levesque. Doesn't he have a place of his own?"

"He likes Mom."

"Everybody likes Mom," Chloe said. "That's why she's never home. But you know what? They're not even going out tonight. They're staying here." She shook her head as if she couldn't quite believe it.

"He's going to make dinner for her. I can't remember the last time a guy wanted to hang around this dump and make dinner for Mom."

"I can," Brynn said.

"Yeah? When?"

"When we were little. When she met Philip Torrence." The brush dropped from Chloe's hand and clattered to the floor.

"Are you trying to tell me something?"

"I already told you," Brynn said. "He likes her. A lot. And I think she likes him."

Chloe groaned. "Not again," she said. "Not a cop."

"You're going to have to clean up your act, Chloe."

Chloe sighed as she stooped to retrieve the brush. "There must be a million guys in this city to choose from. You want to tell me how come she chooses a cop?"

Brynn shrugged. "It's love," she said. "You don't choose it like that. It just happens."

Chloe said nothing. She worked in silence on Brynn's hair for a few moments, then misted the results with hair spray. "There," she said. She stood back to examine her handiwork in the mirror. "What do you think?"

Brynn gazed at her reflection in amazement. She looked so . . . so mature.

"Thanks, Chloe," she said. She threw her arms around Chloe and hugged her.

Chloe squirmed free. "It's no big deal," she said. "If you were half as smart as you think you are, you'd be able to do that yourself."

Brynn laughed. Good old Chloe, she'd never admit she cared.

There was another knock at the front door. Chloe glanced at her watch.

"That's probably Evan," she said. "And I better run or I'm going to be late myself." She started for the door, then turned slowly to face Brynn. "Have a good time," she said. "And really, you look great."

Brynn beamed at the compliment. Coming from Chloe, it meant a lot.

"Good luck at the restaurant," she said.

* * *

Phoebe's hands trembled as she pulled a section of hair around her brush and aimed the blow dryer at it. Her hands had been shaking all day.

Nerves, she told herself. They were jangling in anticipation of the night ahead. She had never been to a dance in her life. And this wasn't just any school dance. It was the prom. The one that girls went to looking like princesses, with boys dressed in suits playing prince. It was normal to be nervous under the circumstances. And it was normal, when you were nervous, for your hands to shake.

But it probably wasn't so normal to have that blinding headache. And it probably wasn't normal for her vision to double and triple in waves, so that she felt she was watching the world from the bottom of a lake. She reached for the aspirin bottle she had kept with her all day, swallowed two more tablets, and continued to blow-dry her hair. As she worked at it, her confidence grew. It was coming out almost exactly like the picture in the magazine. She was going to look stunning. She misted the final result with hair spray and stood back from her mirror. Slowly she turned her head from side to side, so that she could see herself from all angles. Yes, she thought. This is it. I've done it.

She reached for her dress and unzipped it. When she stepped into it and pulled it up, it slid soothingly over her thighs. I've really done it, she thought again, triumphantly. I'm going to the dance and I'm going to look good. Not just good, terrific. Maybe even sensational.

As she slid her feet into her slippers, she heard someone at the front door.

He was here! She could hardly believe the moment had come. A hand rapped gently on her door. "Phoebe?" The door eased open and her mother poked her head into the room. "Bobby's here. Are you ready?"

Phoebe nodded. She had never been more ready. She took one step toward the door before the blackness enveloped her.

* * *

Chloe walked past the restaurant for the second time. She was supposed to have reported for duty five minutes ago, but every time she drew close to the door, her courage failed her. She wished that the judge had arranged it so she and Rita could serve their sentences at the same time. Then she would have company, an ally against the old man. Instead, the judge was forcing each girl to face him alone.

There was no avoiding it. If she didn't go in soon, the old man would complain to the judge and she would get into even deeper trouble. Chloe threw back her shoulders, drew in a deep breath and pushed open the door to the small restaurant. The old man was standing behind the counter. He looked at her, then at the clock on the wall.

"I'm sorry I'm late," Chloe said.

The old man harrumphed.

Chloe approached the counter slowly, her legs trembling. She realized that for once in her life she was afraid. She didn't want to be stuck in this miserable little restaurant all night with an old man who clearly didn't like her. She wished there were some escape.

Out of the corner of her eye she saw the door to the kitchen swing open. Philomen stepped into view.

"Hello, Chloe," he said, smiling at her.

"Hello, Phil," she said. She had been rude to him the last time they'd met, but now, to her surprise, she was relieved to see his friendly face. "What are you doing here?"

"I work here," he said. "I help my grandfather."

Chloe glanced apprehensively at the old man. He was regarding her through narrowed eyes. He hates me, Chloe thought. Then the old man said something to her in Chinese. She didn't understand a word. He said something else. Chloe stared mutely at him. Then, so suddenly that it made her jump, he flung his hands into the air in a gesture of disgust and muttered something to Philomen.

"My grandfather says you are Chinese," Philomen said. "He wants you to speak with him in Chinese."

"I'm not Chinese," Chloe said.

Both Philomen and the old man looked surprised. The old man spoke again.

"My grandfather says you look Chinese."

"I'm not," Chloe said. "I'm only part Chinese."

Philomen translated what he said, and Chloe began to understand how limited his grandfather's grasp of English was. Philomen looked uncomfortable as he listened to his grandfather. He glanced at Chloe, but said nothing.

His grandfather spoke again.

"He wants to know which part," Philomen said.

"My father," Chloe said. "His name was Bertrand Yan." The old man frowned and said something to Philomen.

"He wants to know your father's Chinese name, and the place where his family comes from."

The old man regarded her with such intensity that it embarrassed Chloe to have to say that she didn't know. She saw that the old man wasn't pleased with her answer. She endured a few more moments of his scrutiny before he dismissed her with a wave of his hand and a few gruff words.

"He wants you to start in the kitchen. There are dishes to be washed. I'll show you."

Chloe followed Philomen gratefully into the back

of the restaurant. Anything would be a welcome change from the old man's stare.

* * *

"What's the matter, Chloe? You are so quiet."

Chloe looked up from a sink filled with water and greasy dishes. The old man didn't even have a dishwasher. Everything had to be washed by hand.

"Nothing," she said. "I was just thinking. Why didn't you give the police the pin when you gave them the sweater?"

Philomen looked away and shrugged. "I did not find the pin until later."

"Did you know it was my pin?"

He nodded but still didn't look at her. "I have seen you wear it many times."

"Then why didn't you give it to the police? Why didn't you tell them it was me?"

"Because I . . . I didn't believe you had anything to do with what happened to my grandfather. It was the police who said that maybe the sweater could help them, and I didn't want you to get into any trouble."

Chloe stared at him. "You mean you didn't think I had anything to do with it, even when the police did?"

He shook his head.

"But how did you think the pin got there, for Pete's sake?"

"I thought perhaps you had come into the restaurant because . . . " His voice trailed off.

"Because what?"

"I thought . . . perhaps you came in to see me," he said, the words a hurried jumble. Even his ears were scarlet now, and he grabbed a stack of clean plates and turned away from her to put them on a shelf at the other end of the kitchen.

Chloe looked down at the soapy water. As she plunged her gloved hands into it to locate another plate to wash, she marvelled at Philomen's faith in her, and was ashamed of all the mean things she had said to him. She should be the one whose face was red with embarrassment, not him. As she reached for another plate, she called to him. He turned slowly toward her.

"Phil, I . . . " She hesitated. But there was only one way to do this, and that was straight out — get it over with as quickly as possible. "I'm sorry I've been acting like such a jerk."

The slow shy smile that spread across his face made it almost worthwhile.

* * *

Her mother's worried face floated above Phoebe like a leaf in a pond. When she struggled to sit up, her head pounded. She sank weakly back against her pillow.

"There, there," her mother said. She laid a cool hand against Phoebe's forehead. "Shhh, Phoebe. Rest."

She looked groggily around and realized that she was not in her own room, but in another room, a much larger room, and that a curtain was drawn around her. She also saw that her mother was not alone. Standing just inside the curtain, regarding her with just as much concern, was Levesque.

"You're a sick young lady," her mother said. She caught one of Phoebe's cold hands in hers and squeezed gently. "The doctor says you haven't been eating properly." Then Phoebe remembered her beautiful dress. She looked wildly around. "Don't worry," her mother said. "Your dress is safe."

"Where . . . " Her mouth was so dry that the words stuck in her throat. A wave of embarrassment and self-pity swept over her. She had tried so hard, and everything had been so perfect, but in the end she had done what she always did — she had ruined everything. And what made it worse was that she had done it right in front of Bobby. As she thought of him, tears began to flow. She had ruined Bobby's night. He would probably never ask her out again.

"There, there, sweetie," her mother said. She pressed a tissue into Phoebe's hand. "Dry your eyes. You have a visitor waiting to see you. A very handsome and concerned visitor."

Phoebe's eyes widened. Her hand went automatically to smooth her hair.

"Your hair's fine, Phoebe," Levesque said. "And I don't think you need to worry. If you ask me, this young man likes you for more than just your looks."

Phoebe felt a blush on her cheeks as he pulled the curtain aside and beckoned. She could see Bobby coming toward her from far across the room. She smiled at him.

Turn the page for a preview
of the first Chloe and Levesque
Mystery, *Over the Edge*.

chapter 1

Peter Flosnick wasn't the kind of guy you'd expect to just vanish. I don't know why, but I always figured guys like him liked their lives. Sure, they were outside of things, but they were outside because they were obsessed with, well, whatever they were obsessed with. For some of them, it was computers. For others, mechanical stuff, engines or electronics. For Peter Flosnick it was the stars, as in twinkle, twinkle. He watched them. He studied them. He did science projects about them — award-winning science projects. And he wrote about them in the school newspaper, in an amateur astronomy column that appeared in three different local papers, and in a star-watching column in a kids' magazine. Whenever I saw him around school, he either had his nose in a book — studying up on the history, trajectory or probable life cycle of yet another heavenly body — or in one of those science magazines that are the official badge of nerd-dom. I used to see him around town, too, wandering up a trail in the park or down by the lake, speaking into a pocket-sized tape recorder. I figured, the guy's strange. I also figured he liked it that way — he'd probably keep on being strange until the day he died.

How I found out about Peter's disappearance is this:

I had just dragged myself out of bed — not exactly my favourite activity, I might add. From the top of the stairs I smelled fresh-brewed coffee, bacon and toast. It was the coffee that interested me. I'm a mess without my morning fix of caffeine. When I got there, Phoebe — my younger sister — was sitting at the table, shoving a crust of toast into her mouth. She washed it down with the dregs of a glass of orange juice, then leapt up and dropped a kiss onto Levesque's cheek. He was standing at the stove, frying bacon.

A word about Levesque. Louis Levesque. Mom keeps telling us we should call him Dad, which Phoebe, Little Miss Tell-Me-What-You-Want-and-I'll-Be-Only-Too-Glad-to-Do-It, does. At least Levesque doesn't push the issue. He says I can call him Louis, which I do sometimes. But in my head I always think of him the way he was referred to in the newspapers back home: just plain Levesque. Mom married him a year ago. Two months ago he took a job in East Hastings, and here we are. Some of us — well, me — are not thrilled with his career move. Phoebe loves it here. So does Mom. My older sister, Brynn, escaped exile by graduating high school. She's in CEGEP back in Montreal.

Levesque watched Phoebe race out the door to volleyball practice. An amused smile, barely visible below his bristling moustache, softened his large square face. For a moment he looked like a regular dad on a regular weekday morning, instead of Mr. Officer-of-the-Law, cop-on-duty, the guy with the quickest, sharpest eyes in town. *Look smart, there, pal, I know who you are and I saw what you did.* Then the front door slammed shut and Levesque turned his attention to me.

"Juice?" he said. His tone was pleasant enough, but his eyes were burning into me, as if he were looking for something. He always seemed to be looking for something. I hadn't got used to that yet. That look of his always made me feel guilty, even when I hadn't done anything wrong.

"Just coffee, thanks," I said. I hooked the coffee pot off its warmer pad before he could do it for me.

"Eggs?" he said.

"No, thanks."

"Bacon? Toast?"

"No, thanks," I said again.

"You should reconsider. You know what they say: breakfast is the most important meal of the day."

I dribbled a little milk into my coffee and thought of plenty of things to say, starting with, Hey, Sherlock, have you ever, in the whole year you've known me, seen me eat anything even remotely resembling breakfast? But Levesque could be a pit bull. If I started trying to be smart with him, I could be there all morning. He'd never let go. And besides breakfast, an argument was my least favourite start to the day.

I drank my coffee standing at the sink, looking out the window so that I could make a quick getaway if he decided to keep pestering me with questions. He didn't — he didn't have time to because the phone rang. Levesque handed me the fork, said, "Watch that for me, will you?" and padded across the kitchen floor in sock feet to answer it.

I prodded the sizzling bacon. I would never have admitted it to Levesque, but it sure smelled good. I wondered whether he would notice if I sneaked a piece out of the pan. Probably, I decided. The guy was a detective, after all. Still, my mouth watered, and no matter how hard I tried I couldn't stop thinking how great it would taste to bite down on a strip of crisp, salty bacon.

"Did you talk to his mother?" Levesque was saying into the phone. "Did she have any ideas?" His eyes narrowed and his mouth twisted down, giving his face a look of concentration that I recognized all too well. His cop expression. Whoever he was talking to was talking business. "Okay," Levesque said. "Okay, I'll be right there."

He hung up the phone and disappeared from the kitchen. He was back a moment later with his jacket over his arm and his shoes in his hand.

"You know a kid named Flosnick?" he asked as he tied his laces.

"Peter Flosnick?" It sounds terrible now, under the circumstances, but I remember thinking, what could a mega-nerd like Peter Flosnick possibly have done to get himself in trouble with the police? "I know who he is. Why?"

"He's missing."

"Missing?"

"His mother hasn't seen him since Sunday evening."

This was Tuesday morning.

"Apparently he wasn't at school yesterday, either. You have any ideas?"

"Me?" He had to be kidding. Okay, so I wasn't the big-league joiner Phoebe had turned into — she had signed up for the swim team and the volleyball team, after one debate she had turned into the star of the junior debating team, she had already been elected assistant editor of the yearbook and treasurer of the student council, and for the first time in her life she had zillions of friends. I, on the other hand, was taking a little longer to get my bearings. But that didn't mean I was desperate enough to have a fix on Peter Flosnick's comings and goings. It was just that my friends were back in Montreal, not here.

"I said I know who he *is*," I told Levesque. "But that doesn't mean I know anything about him."

Levesque's moustache twitched, a sure sign he was smiling somewhere under it. "Not your type?" he asked. When I didn't answer he said, "A lot of police work is about asking questions. Sometimes you get lucky and get some answers you can use." He got up and slipped into his jacket.

"What about your breakfast?" I asked.

"No time."

I turned the heat off under the pan, lifted out the bacon strips and set them on a piece of paper towel to drain. The front door clicked shut. I looked at the bacon and took another sip of my coffee. Then I began to eat the bacon one piece at a time.

Thirty minutes later, I was thinking and feeling and wishing the same thing I had thought and felt and wished every weekday morning for the past six weeks.

Look, this is me, standing face-to-face with the enemy and thinking: Shoot me now and put me out of my misery. But, of course, that had already happened. I *had* been shot. Or run over or drowned or dropped off a cliff or fired out of a cannon. I was living in East Hastings, wasn't I, a big pit of nickel and boredom. The bottom line was the same: I had died and now here I was in a town called Hell. (Don't believe me? Take the E from East and the H from Hastings, reverse them and add two L's and what do you get?) I was doomed to tread the same path each and every morning, doomed to end up where I was right now, staring down the enemy. Staring it down and being swallowed up by it all at the same time. There was no escape.

Now this is me looking down at my feet. Looking down at my sneakers and wishing they were ruby slippers. This is me wishing I believed in magic and fairy tales and good witches, wishing I could click my heels together and find myself back home in my own version of Kansas — which for me is Montreal. Okay, so technically Montreal wasn't my home anymore, but it still felt more like home than East Hastings ever would.

Now this is me raising my head and wishing I

would see the big cross that stands on the top of Mount Royal in the middle of Montreal. I used to be able to see it from the front of my old school.

This is me raising my head and actually seeing East Hastings Regional High, built in the style of the nineteen-sixties, with a ratio of brick to windows of about a thousand to one. The school as bunker, designed to keep distractions out, window cleaning bills to a minimum and window repair bills lower still. Twelve hundred kids trudge to and from East Hastings Regional every day. Twelve hundred kids who have no idea what they're missing, stuck up here in a cluster of dots on a map, a handful of little towns that no one in Toronto or Montreal or Vancouver has ever heard of, or, if they have, they can never place. "Where exactly is that?" my friends asked me when I told them where I was going. It's right here, compadres. It's this rinky-dink town where everyone speaks the same language, *ici on ne parle pas français,* where there's no rue St-Denis, no Place d'Armes, no Carré St-Louis, no Gare Centrale, no boulevard René-Levesque, no mountain you can climb to the top of and look out on a sea of twinkling lights. No St. Lawrence River, no Laurentian autoroute, no school trips to ski Mont Tremblant.

And — did I mention this? — there's no escape. Not in the short term. Not that I've discovered. So, here we go, you place one foot in front of the other and repeat as often a necessary until you reach the top of the steps and — whoa! — look at that pair sitting on the wall. How sweet. Just what we all want to see first thing in the morning. Lise Arsenault and Matt Walker, tongue wrestling. They were described around school as an "item." Obviously not an item of good taste.

The bell rang. It was as if the switch on an electromagnet had been flipped, only instead of metal objects, it was kids who were pulled inexorably toward the double front doors. Another day in hell. Or, as we used to say back home, *Ça commence encore.*

That day, for the first time since I had set foot in East Hastings Regional High, I was acutely aware of Peter Flosnick, which was odd, because I had managed to survive almost all of my first six weeks without giving him a single thought. When Ms Michaud read out his name in homeroom, I looked around and saw nothing but indifference reflected in face after face. Nobody seemed to care whether Peter was there to say "Present" or whether his name was followed by silence, signifying absence. Even Ms Michaud didn't pause longer than it took to glance for confirmation at his empty seat. If anyone in the room was thinking, Gee, I wonder where Peter is today, they gave no sign of it. Probably in all of East Hastings only two people cared what had happened to him — his mother, who had called the police, and Levesque, who headed up the police force and was, therefore, responsible for finding him. Poor Peter.

Listen to me. Don't be such a hypocrite, I told

myself sternly. If I ever thought about Peter Flosnick before today, it was only to think what a nerd he was. You can't have such a low opinion of a guy, and then march out an air of superiority when you find yourself the only person who seems to notice when something happens to him. When something *maybe* happens, I amended, because for all anyone knew, he could have stolen a car and gone joy-riding, or run away from home, or maybe bribed someone to score some beer or some hard stuff for him and got fall-down drunk and passed out somewhere, and maybe he's waking up right this minute with a gigantic headache.

Forget Peter Flosnick, I told myself.

* * *

That night after Mom and Phoebe were in bed, I sat up, supposedly reading, but really waiting. It was nearly midnight before I heard the car in the driveway, then the footsteps on the gravelled path that led to the front door. I swung off the bed to the sound of Levesque's keys dropping onto the little table in the front hall. As I tiptoed down the stairs I heard the fridge door open and then close again. Levesque was pouring himself a glass of milk when I entered the kitchen. A bold black eyebrow arched as he glanced from me to the clock on the stove and back at me again.

"Up late studying?" he said. I couldn't tell if it was a serious question or if that annoyingly amused look meant that he suspected I'd been up doing my nails or poring over a teen magazine or something equally frivolous. I could never tell. It drove me crazy sometimes.

"I have a history test tomorrow," I told him.

He nodded and gulped down half of his glass of milk. He wasn't going to volunteer anything. I don't know what had made me think he might. If I wanted to know, I was going to have to ask.

"So," I said, trying to sound casual, "did you find him?"

"Find who?"

"Peter Flosnick."

He drained the rest of the milk from the glass.

"You know I don't discuss police business at home."

I didn't have to be a member of the police detective brotherhood to figure out what that meant.

"So where was he?"

Levesque peered at me for a moment with those coal-black eyes of his. Then he said, "In the park, at MacAdam's Lookout."

MacAdam's Lookout is a cliff. A dizzyingly high cliff. It seems some guy named Jock MacAdam was the first white man to stand on that particular spot and gaze out over what is now East Hastings Provincial Park. The Lookout is solid rock, a big bare slab of Canadian Shield that sticks out like an old man's bald head up above a forest of pine and spruce and birch. There was a certain logic to Peter being there. A guy who loved stars, out in the park, away from the lights of town, where you could get a really good look at the night sky.

"Star-gazing, I bet," I said.

Levesque shook his head. "He was at the bottom of the Lookout, not the top."

That didn't make any sense. "What was he doing there?"

This earned me another long look from Levesque. "I'm sorry to say, he wasn't breathing."

Cover images:
Upper left: First Light/Rubberball
Lower left: First Light/Thinkstock
Right: First Light/A.G.E. Foto Stock